Praise for

HURRICANE CHILD

"The stakes are high, the revelations are serious, and Callender doesn't sugarcoat... But Caroline's insistence on love, no matter what, might be just what young readers need to see."
—*The New York Times*

★ "Set against the richly evoked backdrop of the Caribbean, Callender's novel captures the exquisite agony and pain that accompany rejection and abandonment. Caroline's search for answers provides a steady through line for the story, but it's the deeper questioning and reflection that set this book apart... [T]he inner workings of her mind pay homage to the complexity of being 12. Callender's debut enriches the growing body of LGBTQ fiction for upper-elementary and middle-school students. Visceral, pensive, and memorable." —*Booklist*, **starred review**

★ "Writing in Caroline's present-tense voice, Callender draws readers in and makes them identify with Caroline's angst and sorrow and joy and pain. Embedding their appealing protagonist in a fully realized Caribbean setting, Callender has readers rooting for Caroline the whole way." —*Kirkus Reviews*, **starred review**

★ "Lush descriptions bring the Caribbean environment to vivid life... An excellent and nuanced coming-of-age tale with a dash of magical realism for readers who enjoy character-driven novels, especially those with middle-grade LGBTQ+ characterizations."
—*School Library Journal*, **starred review**

"The immediacy of Caroline's present-tense narration thoroughly immerses readers in an emotional tempest... Callender's debut masterfully deploys the rich landscape of Caribbean life and is trenchant in its portrayal of the cruel reality of prejudice alongside the fragility and resilience of inner strength." —*The Horn Book*

HURRICANE CHILD

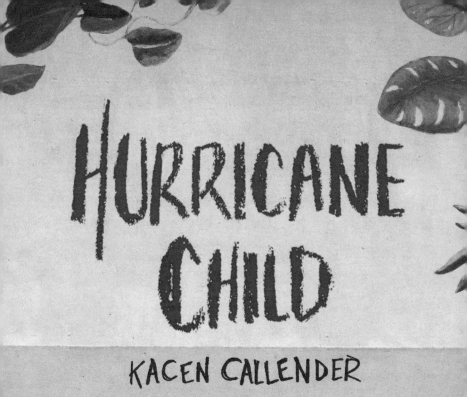

HURRICANE CHILD

KACEN CALLENDER

Scholastic Inc.

For my mother and father,
and the U.S. Virgin Islands

Lyrics from BLACKBIRD
Copyright © 1963, 1964 (Renewed) WB MUSIC CORP.
Words and Music by NINA SIMONE and HERB SACKER
Used by Permission of ALFRED MUSIC

This book was originally published in hardcover by Scholastic Press in 2018.

ISBN 978-1-338-12931-1

10   22 23

Printed in the U.S.A. 40
This edition first printing 2019

Book design by Baily Crawford

THE SPIRITS OF THIS WORLD,
THEY DON'T STAY DEAD FOR LONG.

CHAPTER
1

My ma's voice is rough and low. When she speaks to strangers on the telephone, they call her "sir." I guess it must be surprising to some people, the way her voice sounds, because she's so beautiful—just about the prettiest woman you've ever seen—but I think it suits her just fine. I love the way her rough voice vibrates through the air like a beat on a drum. She sings around the house. Under her breath, since people say her voice is so ugly all the time.

Why you wanna fly, Blackbird?

That's the song that's stuck in my head now.

You ain't ever gonna fly.

*

My dad's blue boat is flipped upside down in the backyard, which isn't really a yard but a grove of dead trees and frogs that won't shut up at night, and the mangrove is just close enough to the water so when it's time to go, I can get out of here with a quickness that will surely inspire the speed of light. My dad hasn't so much as looked at that boat in exactly one year and three months, which is the time that our lives revolve around: one year and three months ago.

The boat's ready, and I'm ready—more ready than ever to get off this dumb rock—but I can't leave yet, because I don't know where to go. But once I do, I'll leave that second without even a good-bye. So I turn my back on my father's boat and walk through the dead mangrove, brown water smelling like something besides the trees died, mosquitoes so thick in the air they might as well be puffs of smoke, dead palms from coconut trees covering the ground like hairy carcasses. I get to the clearing, to the white road covered with dust and gravel and designs of tire marks, to my dad's house that's right there on the edge of the sea, waiting patiently for the day a wave will come and wash it away.

When I was really little—before I started going to school, when I could barely walk without holding my ma's hand—my mom would leave Water Island whenever she needed to go to Saint Thomas for groceries and for church, and she always took me with her. The two of us went on a speedboat owned by Mister Lochana. There was a ferry on the other side of Water Island that could take us to Saint Thomas for ten dollars, but Mister Lochana only charged us five. He was an Indian man that'd come all the way from Tobago, though everyone thought he'd come from Trinidad and called him Mister Trini. I don't know how Mister Lochana felt about that, but I would've corrected each and every single one of them. When I told him so, he laughed.

"To be a child and to be passionate, eh?" he said to my mom.

I asked him, "Does that mean adults aren't passionate about anything?"

My ma told me to hush and sit quiet—I was too little to be running my mouth.

I liked that it was just the three of us, and I liked to look over the side of the speedboat too. I could see the striped yellow and red paint from the boat's side reflected in the clear water, could see the pink coral and stingray, and one day, there was even a fish as big as me. Mister Lochana said it was a nurse shark, and my mom grabbed me and held me so tight I couldn't breathe, even though Mister Lochana promised us nurse sharks don't bite.

One Sunday morning, a wave bumped Mister Lochana's boat high into the air and when it landed again, I fell straight into the water. Since it was Sunday morning, I was wearing a church dress heavy with lace and fake pearls. I fell faster than an anchor, and after I was pulled out again and dragged onto Saint Thomas's concrete, I thought about the bubbles that were bigger than my mom's head, the smoky light that made it hard to see if another nurse shark was coming, the coral that scratched my knees, the woman that was standing on the ocean floor. She was black, blacker than black, blacker than even me. Rough hands yanked me out of the water and hit my chest over and over again until I could breathe.

"You were under there for over a minute, child," Mister Lochana said when I'd opened my eyes. "What was it like?"

All I told him was that the water was deeper than I thought it'd be, and he laughed, though my mom didn't think it was funny. She told Mister Lochana that she wouldn't be using his services anymore, but we ended up in his speedboat again the next week because the ferry to Saint Thomas was too expensive.

*

My dad and I stay in the same house by ourselves. Neither of us want to leave, in case my mom comes back to find the place empty. The outside of the house is painted blue, and the paint gets big bubbles whenever it rains so that I can pick and pick and pick at them until they burst and brown water splashes all down my arm, and there's a pretty little garden with yellow flowers that my mom used to love, but after she left, the flowers have been slowly dying, no matter how much I water them. The house is nice to look at from the ocean too. I used to look at it from my dad's little blue boat, same one I plan on stealing to find my mother. I don't like the ocean too much after I fell out of Mister Lochana's speedboat, but with my dad, I always feel safe. He'd take me in his boat so I could see the fishes swimming in the sea. We had to be careful in that boat, though, because sometimes bigger boats carrying tourists would zoom by and almost hit us like a speedboat hitting a manatee.

One year and three months ago, a little while after my mom left, my dad shook me awake and looked at me with such a smile that I thought Jesus Christ himself must've been standing on our doorstep—or that my mom had come back home.

"Caroline," my dad said. "Wake up, Caroline. There's something you need to see."

He picked me up even though by then I was already eleven and could walk just fine. He took me outside. From his arms I could see the glowing lights. I was scared at first, because by then I'd learned in school about how slaves were sometimes dumped off slave ships before they could even make it to the island. I thought the lights were the ghosts of those slaves coming for me because they were jealous that I'd been born free.

My dad wasn't scared, though. He said they weren't slaves at all but were lost jellyfish—lost, because jellyfish never came to Water Island to glow like that. He put me in his small boat and we drifted out onto the water, waves making us go up and down, and all around us those lights glowed, and it was like the world got confused and turned upside down, and we were floating on the stars, and above our heads were the jellyfish and the sea.

"Almost as pretty as heaven," my dad said. I agreed until I put my hand in the water and got stung so bad I had a rash for days.

*

My dad leaves home three hours before I wake up so he can get to work—that's what he tells me, anyway—so instead of him rowing me across the strip of sea, he takes the ferry by himself, and every morning, I take Mister Lochana's speedboat to the Saint Thomas waterfront.

Sun shines hot and yellow and makes my shirt uniform sticky with sweat. I see the things no one else sees. A woman is standing behind a tree in the shade, watching me, but when I turn my head to say good morning, she's gone again—nothing but the sunshine and baby green leaves swaying in the breeze.

Safari taxis don't like to stop for locals, and the ones that stop for locals don't like to stop for children, so I have to run to catch up with a taxi and jump on just as it slows down for a red traffic light swinging over the street. A woman with big breasts sucks her teeth when I climb over her to squeeze into a little spot without saying excuse me.

It's hot in the safari taxi. The seats are sweaty, and there's no space to breathe, so people stick their heads out the windows. I'm afraid that those heads will get knocked off by trucks in the opposite lanes. The taxi passes by the marketplace, which smells like cooking fish and meat pies, past the baseball fields where children skipping school in their uniforms chase each other and dig through the dirt for soldier crabs. There're the restaurants that smell like the salted stew beef and boiled plantain my mom liked so much. We'd get a plate every Sunday after church, and I always looked forward to the passion fruit juice, so sweet that bees would fly all around me. After she left, I asked my dad if he'd take me to church, and I pretended it was because he'd raised me to be a good Christian girl, but it was really so I could get that juice. He told me we would go the following week, but we haven't gone once since.

Stalls under blue tarp sell fruit and summer dresses and ice-cold rum, and trucks and buses and chickens busily stream by in the granite streets. Across the street, tourists wander off the ferry, snapping photos at the tables of wooden jewelry and fake purses and a donkey named Oprah with her big yellow sunglasses. The taxi slows down in front of a Catholic church, and behind that church is my school.

I leap out of the taxi without paying, since my dad forgot to leave out money again, and I already paid Mister Lochana with all the quarters I could find hidden around the house like in an Easter egg hunt. The taxi driver sees and honks his horn and yells at me in French through his open window. People on the sidewalk look at me as I run right into the middle of the road, cars blaring their horns, chickens squawking at my feet, and up the church steps, my bag smacking my back. I turn around to grin at the taxi driver, who looks like he wants to get out of his safari right then and there to slap me good, and, since I'm not looking, I run right into my teacher, Missus Wilhelmina.

Missus Wilhelmina had a white great-great-great-grandpa from Saint Martin that she likes to talk about all the time because he made her clear-skinned. Missus Wilhelmina says that Saint Thomas and Saint John and

Saint Croix (but not Water Island, because she always forgets about Water Island) and all the other islands in all the Caribbean are no good, seeing that they're filled with so many black people. In class, she says that the Caribbean is almost as bad as Africa itself.

My skin is darker than even the paintings of African queens hanging in tourist shops, same paintings my mom would buy so she could hang them on her living room walls. Their skin is painted with black and purple and blue, and reminds me of the night sky, or of black stones on the side of the beach, rubbed smooth by the waves. I secretly think the women in those paintings are beautiful, but Missus Wilhelmina told me one morning that I have to be a good girl since it'll be hard for me to get married with skin as dark as mine. My dad never says anything like that, but he likes to ask me, "How'd your skin get so dark, Caroline?" Both he and my ma have skin as brown as honey. "How'd you get so dark?"

Seeing that I'm the littlest girl with the darkest skin and the thickest hair in the whole Catholic school, Missus Wilhelmina doesn't like me—no, not at all. I get a smacking on my bum for everything: not looking her in the eye when spoken to, laughing too loud during playtime, thinking I'm better than everyone else because I know the answers to her questions in class, for asking too many questions in class, for not crying after those bum smackings. I always refuse to cry after a bum smacking.

One look at her, and I can tell she saw me jump off that safari taxi without paying.

"Caroline!" she says. "It's always something with you!"

I can't hear her too well after that, since she pinches my ear and wrings it good. She gets an early start on the bum smacking too. She doesn't even wait until she's dragged me into the church. Through the heavy doors, into the heat of the church, down the aisle, Missus Wilhelmina's voice echoes off the walls and bounces into Jesus Christ, hanging from the cross like he always does. He looks down at me with those tired half-closed eyes. It has to be exhausting, hanging on a wall like that all day and all night, listening to so many people's complaints and prayers. He's already going through enough, hanging on a cross, crown of thorns on his head, without having to listen to us too. I'm dragged through the church's back door, which is only ever used by the priest and the choir during service and leads out to the courtyard and classrooms.

The courtyard with its benches and cracked cobblestone ground is spattered with black-and-white bird droppings and filled with green-and-white uniforms and brown legs and shiny loafers, running and screaming and pushing and jumping. There isn't enough room for all of us, so every morning before class we push each other to make enough room—but when Missus Wilhelmina comes, my ear in her hand, the other hand whizzing through the air and landing on my behind, that crowd stops its pushing and parts right down the middle, like how my mom used to part my hair to give me two big braids that poked out the sides of my head.

Missus Wilhelmina yanks me into our classroom of cinder blocks, with ceiling fans pushing hot air around in circles.

"Always something with you," she says again. The doorway she comes through fills with faces and eyes and open mouths. They're funny, pushing one another to see through the door like that, so I laugh.

"You think this is a joke?" Missus Wilhelmina asks.

"Yes," I say.

The kids at the door gasp too loudly. Missus Wilhelmina whips around and sees them there. They scramble away. She turns back to me.

"You don't want to go to this school anymore," she says, "that's what it is. You want to be kicked out of this school."

I agree. "I do."

"You think you're smart," she says, her hand raised again, but I duck.

"Smarter than you," I say, and Missus Wilhelmina chases me out the classroom and into the courtyard, where she gives me a walloping right there, right in front of everyone to see, until the school bell rings and another teacher yells at her to stop before she kills me dead. Missus Wilhelmina is sweating from the effort. She wipes her brow and huffs and puffs.

"Go home," she says, "and don't come back to this school. You hear me?"

That is just fine by me.

*

I do nothing but wander and wander and wander while a little girl no one else can see follows me, skipping along the road, and when I get home long after the sun's gone down, my dad sits on the sofa, looking as tired as the Jesus Christ that hangs on the church wall. He tells me he just got off the phone with my principal, who will let me come back to school tomorrow—as if this is something that should make me grateful.

"Did you hear me, Caroline?" he says. "You can go back to school tomorrow."

I don't speak. I don't tell him about Missus Wilhelmina, or say he forgot to leave money on the counter again. If my mom were here, I wouldn't have to say anything at all. She would just sit me down on the floor in front of the couch so my shoulders pressed into her hard, round knees, and she would take a thin comb and undo my plaits while she sang a song so low under her breath that I could never tell what she was singing, not at first, and even though a cartoon would be on I'd strain my ears to listen to my mother's voice instead.

'Cause your mama's name was lonely.

The day she left and didn't take me with her, I

decided I would find her again. Remind her that I was Caroline Murphy, her only daughter, and that she loved me too much to leave me behind. Then she would laugh and say it was her mistake, and take me into her arms, and even though most people always wanted to let go after just a few seconds, my mom would only stop hugging me when I told her to, and if it were up to me, she'd just keep holding on forever.

"Caroline—where're you going? I'm not done speaking to you—"

I get to my room before my dad can reach me, and slam and lock the door with such a quickness I know he must wonder how his little girl got to be so fast. I sit on the edge of my bed, feet too big on the sheets, knees hugged to my chest as he knocks on the door gently, politely, telling me to come back out again. Then he hammers and yells and says I'm a little brat, and he has enough to worry about already. Then he just stands there, breathing. I only come out again when I hear him leave the house for work in the morning.

CHAPTER 2

One morning my mom got up and went halfway across the world, as my dad likes to say. She sent postcards from all the places she traveled to, names of cities I couldn't even pronounce, but the postcards stopped coming after the ocean got up and killed all those people, and for a while my dad thought my mom was dead too. Then the cards started coming again, from small towns across Europe, but the handwriting was scratched quickly, and my mom had less to say with every new postcard, with every new town. When the cards stopped coming again, it wasn't because my dad thought my mom was dead.

Opening the mail in the morning became a ritual. The two of us, my dad and me, sitting at the kitchen table like we were about to say a prayer before a feast, him ta... ...letters and bills from the post office and o... ... ...ging ...y feet while I waited for ...im to find a post...rd slipped in between—but after the fifty-third morning since we got the last post-card, my pa put the letters down in a neat stack after opening them and told me, "I don't think we'll be hearing from your mother again for a while, Caroline."

That's all he said about it. He stood up from the table, chair scraping the yellow tile, while I bit my lip. He went to the stove, pots clanging. I kept swinging my feet.

And your daddy's name was pain.

And I knew it before. Knew it then. Still know it now.

I have to find her.

*

I know something's wrong when I get to school the next morning and a little girl with twists in her hair stands in the middle of the aisle of the church. When she sees me, she jumps right up into the air and turns tail and runs for the door at the back of the church, screaming, "Caroline Murphy is here! Caroline Murphy is here!" so loud that I'm afraid Jesus Christ and his cross will fall right off the wall.

I don't know what they have planned, but I'm no coward, so I go right down that aisle out the back door and into the hot courtyard. A half circle is waiting for me like a mob that's ready to burn me at the stake. They're all holding stones.

"Why don't you have a mom anymore, Caroline?" a girl asks. I know her well. Anise Fowler. Her hair is ironed straight, and some days I think I can still smell it burning. Her nails are always painted because her mom takes her to the spa. Today they're scarlet red.

She's waiting for me to speak. They're all waiting for me.

"I still have a mom," I tell them.

"Heard she ran off with another man."

I don't know if she actually heard that, or if she's just making it up. "She didn't," I say.

"You're gonna be just like her," Anise says. "You're gonna run off with some man."

"Same way your mom did?" I ask, since this is openly spread knowledge—something that everyone whispers, because they heard it from their parents, though no one ever says it to Anise's face.

Anise's smile twitches. She doesn't need to give a signal. They all know to start throwing the rocks right then and there. They're small enough that they won't kill me, but chunks of mud dirties my white-collared shirt, and sharp pebbles scratch my ears and my cheeks and my knees and my hands when I reach out to protect my eyes. Anise is aiming right for my eyes.

When they run out of rocks, I look at my hands. Both are speckled red, and points of blood start to rise and dry. I look at those smiling faces all around me, and I reach down for the rocks at my feet and I pick them up and throw them as hard as I can at each and every one of them, even the ones who'd only been watching. They scream and scatter except for Anise, and I pick up the biggest rock I can find and aim it right at her head. It knocks her above her eye, and she falls to the ground.

Three teachers, with Missus Wilhelmina right up front, come hurrying into the courtyard. Piles of dirt and rocks everywhere, and me in the middle, with my hair sticking out of its braids and dirt all down my front and little children pointing at me, telling those teachers I'm the one who threw the rocks.

*

"I will not force you to leave this school, Miss Murphy," the principal says. I'm sitting on my hands in her cramped, sweltering office, which has shelves covering every wall, each stuffed with piles of books and loose papers looking ready to whip around the room in a windstorm. There are so many books and papers I'm afraid they're all going to come crashing down on my head. The principal doesn't seem to be scared at all. Miss Joe is her name, and she only ever calls students by their last names, because she says then we will know we are destined for excellence, though I'm not sure what my last name has to do with anything.

"I believe that you are an angry little girl, and that you're angry because you've been hurt, and that you need help to overcome this pain, and so I could not force you to leave this school with a good conscience. However," she says, "you now have two strikes against you. If you do something like this again, I'm afraid I will have no choice."

There's a spider inspecting its web up in the corner of her office. Miss Joe stands from her seat with difficulty, since the books are everywhere, teetering on the edge of her desk and their shelves and threatening to fall to the floor. She carefully comes to a stop beside me and my chair.

"Every little girl needs her mother," she says, and that's all she says about that before she pulls out a book from her shelf. I don't know how she knows where to find it, but her hand shoots straight for it and yanks it out of its pile. The book has a purple leather cover with a gold hibiscus flower embossed on the front. She flips through it, tears out a few pages, then hands the book to me. It has fancy paper that is thick and yellow, with golden flowers designed in the corners. I decide it's the prettiest paper I've ever seen.

"You should write letters to your mother," she says, "and one day—if you do meet her again—you can decide whether you would like to give these letters to her or not."

I take the journal and say thank you, because my ma always taught me to say thank you if anyone ever gave me something, but I already know I won't be writing a single word on any of this paper. It's the first gift I've gotten from someone who is not my mom or my dad, and I plan on keeping it preserved on my nightstand, pretty paper untouched.

Miss Joe smiles. "Just don't throw any more stones," she tells me.

*

One day before the stone throwing, I sat by myself in the classroom of precise desks and chalk dust, and I sat alone during lunch too, just like I always have, in the small, hot cafeteria of sticky tiles and plastic tables stained with spilled fruit juice, and with wood slave salamanders with their translucent skin letting anyone see their guts as they skittered across window screens. I watched the students who would not come near me or look at me because I got so many bum smackings and because I asked too many questions in class and because I knew too many answers too. They never paid me any mind. I might as well have been invisible, because everyone else would always walk right by, laughing and teasing each other and going to sit at the tables where they always sat. No one would ever say, "Come and join us, Caroline," so I would then spend the rest of the lunch period feeling sorry for myself and trying to remember that the lonely children like me are the ones who grow up to be someone that everyone wishes they could be.

One day after the stone throwing, nothing has really changed, except now those children watch me watching them. They lean into their friends to say something and then their friend laughs. Anise sits on the other side of the cafeteria, but I can hear her voice over the hum of talk.

"That Caroline Murphy is a female dog," she says, except she doesn't say *female dog*, but the rude word my mom would've slapped me silly for saying. "Look what she did to my head. I had to get stitches, and now they say there will be a scar. I suppose that's what happens when you're not raised the right way." And her friends tsk and shake their heads the same way they've seen their mothers do over meals of lemongrass tea and salt fish and fungi.

There is one girl who watches me watching her, but she does not look at me in the angry way everyone else does. She is white, and she is Anise's friend and sits at the table where Anise sits, but I've never seen her speak before in my life. I think she might be deaf, or mute, or chooses not to say a single word, the same way the Chief refuses to speak in *One Flew Over the Cuckoo's Nest*, which I only know about because it's one of the books my mom read aloud for me at night, me curled up next to her in her soft bed, always begging for her to keep reading even after her voice was scratchy and hoarse, and hating my dad whenever he opened the door and told me to go to my own room because he wanted to sleep.

Marie is her name, but everyone calls her Marie Antoinette because she's white. She has yellow hair and blue eyes and looks the way the rest of the world thinks everyone should always look, since people with yellow hair and blue eyes are supposed to be more beautiful than anyone else, even though no one can see that they were brainwashed into thinking only yellow hair and blue eyes are beautiful, on account of the fact that people with yellow hair and blue eyes did the brainwashing themselves, so the moment I saw Marie I decided I didn't like her, since everyone automatically likes her for looking the way she does, and everyone automatically hates me for looking the way I do.

I still don't like her, but while Anise is talking loud, Marie Antoinette keeps looking at me silently, and every time our eyes meet she looks back down at the table again. She looks again at me, and then again and again, until by the end of lunch, I've caught her looking at me nearly sixteen times. That's a lot of times to look at someone, so I figure she must want something from me. I decide to ask her about it directly, instead of spending the rest of the day wondering.

"Hello," I tell Marie in the hallway. My hands are shaking, so I clasp them behind my back where no one will see. Anise is close enough to spit in my face, and she might just do it too, after she's done twisting up her face in shock and disgust.

Marie looks surprised also. She nods her head at me.

"I wondered if you would like to take a walk after school," I tell her, since I know she lives in Frenchtown, where a lot of white people live on Saint Thomas, which is right next to waterfront.

Marie hesitates, then looks at Anise and her other friends, then looks at me again and shakes her head. She walks away, and Anise laughs loudly, then begins to demand to her friends, "What does she think she's doing? Who does she think she is?" And even then, though Marie smiles with the rest of them, I see her looking down the hall at me, over her shoulder, like she's trying to telepathically send me a message, but I'm just not tuned into the right station to hear it.

*

When I get home, my dad still hasn't returned from work. I toe off my shoes and socks and leave them in a pile by my bedroom door like I always do, and I see the journal that Miss Joe gave me yesterday on my nightstand. I pick it up, thinking that maybe I will write a letter to my mom after all—but then I throw it as hard as I can, so hard that it knocks into a lamp that my mother said was *exquisitely beautiful* the second she saw it, and bought it immediately, and surprised me when she took it to my room instead of placing it on display in the living room for everyone to see. The lamp crashes to the floor into a million little pieces, so tiny that parts have become powder.

I could fall to my knees and cry right then, but crying won't do a single thing, so instead, I run out of the house, screen door slapping shut behind me, and run barefoot through the brown salt water, splashing over roots and cutting my toes on stones, until I reach my father's blue boat. I take a deep breath and heave and yank and tug until my arms feel like water and my legs buckle beneath me, and I'm sweating in the evening heat, and mosquitoes get tangled in my hair, but I don't stop until that boat is sitting right side up again. I take another breath and push and push and push until it's right there by the water's edge. I don't know where I'm going, don't know where my mom is, but it doesn't matter—I decide the waves will take me to her. I leap inside and feel the water bob me up and down, up and down. And just as I grab the paddles, I see her sitting there—sitting across from me like an old friend whose name I don't recall.

She has eyes shining like two full moons in her face, but everything else is black, and I can't really see her at all, as though she only ever exists in the corner of my eye—and she's gone the moment I turn my head to get a good look at her.

I sit there, listening to the gentle plunk of water smacking the bottom of the boat, looking out at the ocean that has opened itself before me, still and flat like black glass. She's already gone, but I whisper, "Is that you, Mom?"

Nothing answers but the trade winds rustling through my hair. The woman in black is long gone, but I can still feel her near me. I hear my father shouting my name. "Caroline! Caroline! Caroooline!"

I jump out of the boat, feet sinking into the salt water and sand that sting the cuts on my toes, and push the boat back through the mud of the dead mangrove, until it finds solid dirt again. By the time I wander back to my father's house, I'm covered in mud and tears. He's waiting on the top of the stairs, light of the house shining through the screen door. I think he will yell at me, and for a moment, he probably thinks the same—but then he sees me and opens his arms to me and holds me, smoothing down my hair almost the same way my mom would have

28

done. He doesn't hold me until I ask him to let go, but I still can't help but love him for it.

And I feel bad, because I know I'm going to leave him here in this house by himself, same way my ma left the two of us.

CHAPTER
3

I am a Hurricane Child. It doesn't mean anything special, except that I was born during a hurricane. My ma told me this story at least once a month, but sometimes twice, whenever she was extra in love with me, in a mood where her love was so big I was scared she'd crush me with it, and she wanted to share that love with me by remembering my birth, so I had the story practically memorized—not only the words, but even when she would pause and close her eyes and let her mouth twist into a smile.

It was her favorite story to tell. She wasn't expecting me that night, but same way you can't always expect someone to just up and die and leave this world, I jumped right into it a whole month early. She'd smile. My dad, being a good man, was down the road helping the old women tie down their roofs and board up their windows, and even though technology existed, sometimes Water Island might as well have been stuck in the old world with a magic barrier keeping everyone and everything out, so even though my ma screamed and screamed and screamed, not a soul heard her.

She filled the bathtub with warm water and lowered herself into it, and she was there in that water while the storm spun into the islands faster than anyone expected, lashing the house with rain and wind that blew the kitchen window right inside and brought the sea up into our house so the water was near up to a grown man's knees, and whenever I asked my ma, she said she was more than positive that it wasn't just a hurricane but a water sprout too, a twister born on the ocean and flying up onto land to die, same way some insects are born and die all in the same second sometimes.

She'd clench her hands. My dad, my mother said, was stuck down the road, hiding with one of the old women under her kitchen sink, but the second the water twister stopped roaring, he leapt up and ran through that storm to find us—both my mom and me sitting in a tub of bloody water. Even though it was a whole month early, I might as well have been in her stomach a year, I was so big and loud, wailing over the wind and rain. Almost like I didn't really belong in this world. Hurricane just tore me from the spirit world and spat me out into this one instead. She'd kiss my cheek and touch my hair.

My mom never told me what it means to be a Hurricane Child. She never put that in her story. But I hear what it means when the old women from down the road come by, from their dead friend who whispers it under her breath. That it's a curse, being born during a hurricane. I won't have an inch of luck for the rest of my days, and sadness will follow me wherever I go.

And he called you little sorrow.

Well, I step on that curse and spit on it too.

I don't need this world's luck to live. I don't even need anyone to like me.

I've just got to focus on one thing: finding my ma. That's all I'll ever need.

*

My ma and I would sometimes sing at the top of our lungs like we didn't care if everyone in the world could hear us, and together, we would sing calypso and soca and old-time reggae, but alone, she would sing her softer songs.

Why you wanna fly, Blackbird?

I don't know anything about blackbirds, because I've never seen one with my own eyes, but I know that I am one all the same. When we sang as loud as we could, my mom would pick me up and swing me over her head and I would scream and we'd both near fall with laughing. Knew I'd never be loved again as much as when I was loved by my mother. Never be loved that way again.

*

The very last time my mother was not so close to me that she could touch, but she was still closer than she is now, is when she was sending those postcards. And I think that maybe the very last postcard she sent is exactly where she is now.

My father did not throw those postcards away. I know that he has stored them in a room that no one sleeps in, beside the gardening tools and old books, stacks of picture books and board books that my mother used to read to me. There are bins of unused cards. She used to buy cards in advance and would collect HAPPY BIRTHDAY cards and CONGRATULATIONS! cards and I'M SORRY FOR YOUR LOSS cards so she would always be prepared for a forgotten birthday or an unexpected passing.

The bins are filled with these cards, but I don't see my mother's postcards anywhere, so I look and look and look and uproot the bins, and when I've gone through every single last card, I look inside the picture books too, in case the cards have been used as bookmarks, and I look behind the gardening tools and inside the cupboards and try not to cry with how frustrated I am. My hands are covered with paper cuts. And finally, I sit back and admit that the postcards are nowhere to be found.

My father appears behind me, concern on his face. "Caroline, what're you doing?"

I wasn't expecting him, and he's scared me so much that my heart is beating like a hummingbird's wings and is warm in my chest, the way it is when I suddenly shoot up in my bed, awake with fear from a nightmare. "I'm looking for something."

"I can see that. What're you looking for?"

I hesitate. If I told him, would he realize I'm looking for my mom? Or would he simply show me where he's stored the postcards?

I decide to take a risk. "I'm looking for the postcards Ma used to send us."

"Oh." He crosses his arms. "Why would you want those?"

I open my mouth, and a lie slips out before I've even had a chance to think of one. "I have a school project about world geography, and I thought I would choose one of the countries she traveled to."

"Oh," he says again. "Well, I threw those cards away a long time ago."

I try to stop the disappointment that crashes down around me, but I must not do a very good job, because my father gives me a smile and helps me to my feet. "I have some ideas for countries to do a project on," he says. "There are many countries I've been to."

This isn't something I knew about my father. I've

known my father my entire life, and he knew me even before my life began, so it's a funny notion, that I still have to get to know him.

*

Missus Wilhelmina's classroom is alight with excitement the next morning. That kind of excitement never bodes well for me. Usually the heads bent together and sharp spikes of laughter mean that Anise has something planned. I step inside, expecting everyone to start throwing books at my head, but I breathe with relief when their gazes barely flicker to me. *Breathe with relief*—that almost makes me sound afraid. I hate being afraid. I hate being a coward. I decide I'll never breathe with relief again.

Ignored by everyone, I sit in my assigned desk and listen to the whispers around me.

"Have you seen her?"

"She looks wild."

"I hear she's from Barbados."

It's barely enough information, but I piece it together: Someone new is joining the class. Our school is so small that the last new student we ever had was about four years ago, and it was a girl who only came for a day, before she began to cry and sob and wail, snot dripping down her front and all, and she had to be picked up by her mother before recess even began, and we never saw her face again.

Missus Wilhelmina steps inside then, and everyone falls into a church-like silence—they've all seen my bum smackings enough to fear her. Her expression is pinched today, like she's walked into a room to discover a forgotten ham covered with maggots, which is just what happened over Thanksgiving vacation just one year before. She folds her hands in front of her stomach.

"Class," she says in her nasally voice, as though she's smelling that rotten ham too, "we have a new student joining us. Please welcome Kalinda Francis."

A girl walks in. The heads swerve. I lean out of my desk to get a better look. I can barely see her between the first few rows. Even with Missus Wilhelmina standing there, the excited whispers break out again, and Anise says something that makes her group of hyenas howl. Missus Wilhelmina stands taller and straighter until the room quiets down once again.

"Say hello, Kalinda," Missus Wilhelmina whispers, tone dripping with disgust.

All I can see are scarred brown knees and white socks and shining black loafers, but the voice that comes out nearly sounds like a grown woman's—it's deep and grave. "My name is Kalinda Francis, and I am twelve years old." Kalinda might as well be speaking at a funeral, she sounds so serious.

Missus Wilhelmina tells Kalinda to take a seat in the front row beside Marie Antoinette. It's only then that I see her hair: thick locks, twisted and braided together and piled on top of her head so high it's a wonder they don't snap her neck! My mouth falls open at the sight of her, and I'm not the only one staring. If Kalinda notices, she doesn't seem to pay us any mind. She takes her seat as she's told and holds her head so high and proud that she reminds me of the paintings of African queens my mother left hanging on our living room wall.

When Missus Wilhelmina turns her back to start her lesson, Anise begins to whisper from her second row. "I heard that Rastas don't wash their hair, so they have caterpillars living in their locks. Did you hear that one story about that Rastafarian from Tutu? He had a horrible headache one morning, and so he went to the doctor, but the doctor couldn't find anything wrong with him, so he went home again, but his headache just kept getting worse and worse, until finally one day he fell down dead! When the doctor looked at him again, he saw that a spider living in the man's hair had laid a nest, and that it had burrowed into the Rasta's skull to do it."

There are squeals and laughs all around. Missus Wilhelmina would usually whip around and clap her hands together and demand that the perpetrator stand outside in the hot courtyard for the rest of the lesson (unless it was me—if it was me, then I would get a walloping right then and there), but today she only continues to scratch her chalk against the chalkboard. Everyone looks to Kalinda, to see if she has heard Anise's story about this Rastafarian, and what she will do about it if she has.

Kalinda does not pretend she didn't hear. She looks at Anise with interest. "I knew that man," she says. "He was my uncle."

Anise's eyes become big, and there's a collective intake of breath around the room—but then Kalinda smiles and looks at the chalkboard again, and it's clear that she was only joking, and the room erupts with giggles that Missus Wilhelmina finally can't ignore. She turns around and hushes us all and stamps her foot until we're quiet again.

I decide then and there that Kalinda would make a great candidate for the first friend I've ever had. Anyone brave enough to stand up to Anise like that—well, maybe she'd be brave enough to stand up to the rest of my class too, and would realize that they were silly and mean, and the two of us would sit together for lunch every afternoon and walk to waterfront after school, and everyone would realize what a good a friend I am—so good that they'll want me to like them too, and suddenly I'd find everyone talking to me and asking me and Kalinda Francis to join them at their lunch tables.

A new student. It's like a dream, almost, to be seen by someone who has never looked at you before, someone who is not the same thirteen classmates you've had all your life, someone who is not your teacher or a parent, someone who does not know who you have been and has not already decided who you are, or what you will become. It's more than a chance to create a new identity. It's a chance to really become someone else—or, perhaps, to really become myself.

And for me, it's the only chance I'll ever have.

But halfway through class, I see Anise write a note and slip it to Kalinda. Kalinda turns, surprised, and reads the note, then smiles and nods. An invitation to eat lunch with Anise, Marie Antoinette, and the other hyenas, no doubt. I shouldn't be surprised. There's no way they would ever let Kalinda sit anywhere else after that scene. Even if Anise doesn't like Kalinda or any other Rastafarian, it's clear that everyone in this school will soon want to be Kalinda's friend, and so Anise must get to her first. Before I know it, the first chance I've ever had at making a friend is gone before the first class period has even ended.

*

I see the things no one else sees. As I'm walking to the cafeteria, out the classroom and into the courtyard, there's a white woman standing in her nightgown, standing across the yard, away from a crowd of fuzzy black hair and green-and-white uniforms, and the closer I get, the more I see that they're all standing around one person—Kalinda. The white woman is watching Kalinda too, but the next second I blink and she's gone and there's nothing but a dead rosebush standing where she was.

Students are speaking around Kalinda loudly, buzzing with anticipation, and whenever there's a break in the noise, I can tell even from where I stand, it's because Kalinda is speaking. I want to hear what she has to say. Her voice is so serious, so grave, I'm positive that anything she has to say must be important. She's probably the one and only person in this entire school we all need to listen to.

I hesitate by the doorway. I want to join the group, stand with them and listen to what Kalinda is saying, but Anise and Marie Antoinette and others are also gathered around, and I don't know what they'll do. If they'll say something that will make me feel ashamed in front of Kalinda, if they'll immediately let her know that I'm the most hated girl of this school, warning her to never speak to me so Kalinda Francis will start to look at me with disgust too.

The group lets out one long, hard laugh, and I decide that it's a risk I'm willing to take. I walk to the group and stop behind them, standing on my toes to see inside of the circle. Kalinda has let down her locks out of their twists to show just how long they are. They reach the back of her bum!

I must have gasped, because the next second, Anise looks at me, and her face turns into such disgust that it's clearer than ever that she thinks I never should've been born.

"Hasn't something started to stink?" she asks Marie Antoinette, who looks around in confusion, until she sees me and then nods. She chooses to say this specifically, because just a few months before, it became apparent that a horrible smell had begun to ooze from my skin, so much so Missus Wilhelmina one day pulled me to the side and told me that I need to wear more deodorant.

Anise has already tortured me enough by reminding me of my stink whenever I get too close, and now when she says this, I'm not sure if it's because it's true. The others around her see me, and then pinch their noses and wave the air in front of their faces impatiently, and there's Kalinda in the middle of all of them, looking right at me. I begin to wish that I'd never been born either. I turn on my heel and try to walk slowly, like I don't care that they're all staring after me and laughing, like I don't care one bit at all.

*

Visitors come to Water Island. I see the things no one else can see, but I'm not sure anyone else can see the visitors too. They take a house that's on the other side of Water Island's brown hill. Water Island has a scarred hill, big brown scorch mark shining like a giant leech, because one day during Carnival almost seven years back, fireworks went off over the Saint Thomas waterfront and exploded right above us, even though fireworks were only ever supposed to explode over the sea. My mom was still home, and she wanted me to go to bed so if the fire came for us, I wouldn't see death coming—but my dad took my hand and together we went out to see. I was five years old, and I thought the sun was falling down. I fancied myself brave, because I was standing my ground and looking that sun right in the eye.

Helicopters came and dumped buckets of seawater on the hill, so my mom and my dad and I stayed alive, but by then the house on the very top of the hill was burned and the man who lived there had died. My mom said that children are children because they know nothing about death, so I guess that day I stopped being a child. They left the skeleton of his blackened house behind as a gravestone. It stayed there until the hurricane took that away too.

Water Island is supposed to be a part of the United States Virgin Islands, but we were never sainted like Saint Thomas or Saint John or Saint Croix, and so everyone forgets we exist. People have forgotten about Water Island since the days when there were slaves. Since no one remembered Water Island was right there beside Saint Thomas, slaves escaped to Water Island to be free. They didn't have to hide whenever a boat filled with white men passed by because those men never even looked their way. I guess some of the slaves started to believe that the island was magic—magic so no one could see its hills except the people who already knew it was there. No one knows who the magic belongs to, but it's stayed all these years, so I'm invisible whenever I'm on Water Island too, and that suits me just fine. Nobody ever looks my way anyway.

The house on the other side of the brown hill has been available for rent since before I was born, but since Water Island is always forgotten, no one has ever come to stay there before. I notice those visitors on the ferry docks, down the road from Mister Lochana. It's a girl with her mother. She's younger than me by years, and when she sees me, she doesn't look away. She has my pa's nose.

The first night the visitors are on Water Island, I go for a walk so I can see them in the house they rented behind the hill. Before I can even get close, that girl sees me from the porch. She watches me good until I leave again.

*

The girl with my dad's nose starts coming down the road. She has skin that's honey brown like my dad's too. She'll just stand in the shade of the kenep trees, watching me whenever I leave for Mister Lochana's. I don't say anything about her to my dad, but one day she's standing directly outside my house. Her legs are covered in red mosquito bites, and her teeth are too big for her mouth.

"Hello," she says. "My name is Bernadette."

I decide that I don't like Bernadette very much. "Why would I want to know something like that?"

"Your name is Caroline."

Now she has my attention. "Who told you that?"

She doesn't answer me. She continues to stare with her eyes that seem to get bigger in her face, like inflating balloons. She leans down to scratch at a mosquito bite.

"You shouldn't scratch," I tell her.

"But it itches."

I just cross my arms. She tells me her birthday, which is the same day my mom left me to travel halfway across the world one year and three months ago, and that she came here to meet my father, who she says is also her father. I run away from her before she can think of another word to say to me, slamming shut the screen door so hard it bounces open again.

Inside my house, I keep looking at my dad, expecting him to say something about the visitors—but he just keeps sighing like he's a man who knows that death is coming, just a few more years, nothing he can do about it now.

"Daddy," I tell him, because I always call him *Daddy* to his face so he'll think I love him more than I really do, "who is the girl who moved into the house behind the hill?"

He sighs again, like me being in front of him is bringing death even faster. I don't think he wants to speak to me about Bernadette.

"Daddy," I say again, "do you know where my ma is?"

This makes him look at me in a way I've never seen him look at me before. Like I am no longer the little girl he would toss into the air and catch again, or the little girl he would perform magic tricks for, holding a ball in his hand one second and then revealing an empty palm the next, or the little girl he would take out on his boat so we could get lost in the sea and the stars. No—now he looks at me like he has realized I am no longer a child at all. This is a realization I had many years ago, when Water Island was set on fire, but I've never showed the truth to him before. I'm showing it to him now. Just by asking him such a question, I can see that my pa has realized I'm not a little girl.

I ask him again. "Where is my mom?"

My mother always sent us postcards of the cities she had gone to, so I never had to ask where she was—it was written there for us to see. After the postcards stopped coming, I was too angry to ask. But I'm asking now—again, a third time, to be sure he's heard me. "Where's my mom?"

Except this time, I've also added a word I should never use when speaking to my father, not when he's the man that's partly responsible for my existence, the reason I even get to be here speaking and breathing. He slaps my cheek with a quickness and looks just as shocked as I do, and in that moment I decide I want nothing more to do with my father—nothing more to do with him ever again.

CHAPTER
4

Days go by where I don't speak. I will not answer my father when he tells me good evening after I've returned home from school. Missus Wilhelmina is glad for my silence in her classroom, and the other students were never speaking to me anyway. I only ever bother to nod my head politely to Mister Lochana in the early mornings. We zoom across the clear water, and overhead the birds fly, and there are sea turtles too, drifting through the clouds.

As a deaf man might have better eyesight, or a blind man can hear so much more, I feel an extra sense growing. One where I can know another person's thoughts or feelings without them ever having to open their mouths. Such as when the sunlight glints in Marie Antoinette's yellow hair, and Anise looks at her with the anger of a cat being woken from a nap, or when Missus Wilhelmina stares out the window while we do our quiet reading, and she looks as though she might be a bird that can take flight at any moment, escaping into the endless blue sky. I decide that I like my silence, and that maybe I should run away to become a monk so I will never have to speak to anyone ever again.

But then Miss Joe calls me into her office during lunchtime that very day, and I know she'll expect me to break my vow.

"How are you doing today, Miss Murphy?" she asks.

I don't speak.

She turns her head to the side inquisitively over her tall pile of books. It almost looks like she's a child who decided to build herself a fort. "Are you all right, Miss Murphy?"

Here, I nod my head.

She takes a breath, her shoulders raised into a shrug. "Well, I must say, I'm worried about you. You seem to be a very lonely little girl."

She might as well have spit in my face. This is such an insulting thing to hear that I wouldn't have been able to think of anything to say anyway, even if I were letting words out of my mouth.

I expect her to go on with her insult, to explain why she thinks I'm a lonely little girl (even if she is right)—but instead she takes another breath. "I know your mother."

And here, I'm not proud to say, I break my vow— immediately, without even a pause of hesitation. "What do you mean, you know my mother?"

"Doreen Murphy," she says. "Doreen Hendricks, when she was little. Would you like to hear more about her?"

I nod. I don't need to be silent to see the salt that begins to shine in Miss Joe's eyes.

*

Miss Joe calls home to let my father know that I'll be going to her house for dinner tonight. She drives a red pickup truck, and in the back are bundles of fruit she picked for herself: kenep with juices leaking from the pits, and mangoes that remind me of miniature suns, and brown plantains so brown they look rotten. She lets me sit in the front of the truck, and the broken leather scratches my thighs, and the seat stuffing spills out and tickles my skin. Miss Joe turns on the radio so old people's music begins to play, and she sings along loudly so I don't feel like I have to be polite and start talking about stuff that doesn't matter. She reaches behind her and pulls out a sliver of sugarcane and hands it to me, and her eyes smile at me, though her lips just keep on singing their tune.

The sugarcane is sticky, and I chew it so hard that it hurts my teeth. Cars race by, zooming in front of Miss Joe, and usually taxi drivers would cuss and throw up their hands whenever a car zooms in front of them like that, but Miss Joe just goes on singing her songs. She turns a corner and drives into a market that makes me roll up the window to keep out the stink of dead fish. Miss Joe points out the woman standing in the shade of the post office and tells me she is ninety years old, and for a second I think she's the woman in black, her skin is so dark, but no—she's just a woman hiding from the sun.

And then it hits me, what Miss Joe said. Ninety years old? I can't even imagine being twenty, let alone ninety, and I'm already positive that I won't live past sixteen, because I'm more than sure that this world will never let me live to an important age like that, and everyone will have to come to my funeral and cry about how they treated poor little Caroline Murphy, and beg my spirit for forgiveness (which I'll give out of the mercy of my heart)—but maybe in the same way that I can't imagine being ninety, this woman looks at sea turtles and thinks she cannot imagine being two hundred years old, and maybe the sea turtle looks at our islands and thinks he cannot imagine existing since the beginning of time.

Miss Joe stops the truck on the side of the road, right under a sign that says NO PARKING. A girl even smaller than me runs toward us before she bursts into moths that fly into my hair and make me near jump right out of my skin. Miss Joe takes no notice. She walks me down a side street where no car can fit. The path is paved with cement, and there are wild roses on either side, so long that the thorns threaten to scratch my arms. At the end of the path is a one-story house made of rotting wood, even though most houses in the Virgin Islands are made of concrete so they won't be blown away by the hurricanes.

*

Here is what I know about Miss Joe: She doesn't have a husband, and she doesn't have any children of her own. Just from listening to what the other children at school say, I know that not many mothers like Miss Joe. They say she's a woman that isn't really a woman at all, but is a snake in disguise. When her red pickup truck breaks down, she doesn't have a man to call, so she fixes it herself. When she's thirsty or hungry, she cooks for herself and only herself, not for a husband asking for this and that. She's like the slaves back in the day who weren't really slaves at all because they'd taken their freedom, and lived in their own houses, and owned their own clothes, and ate their own food. People didn't like seeing slaves like that, and people don't like seeing a woman like that now either. It makes those people even madder when Miss Joe stands so tall and reads big books and talks like she has not a care in the world. I decide in that moment that I want to be precisely like Miss Joe, and I stand a little straighter.

Miss Joe takes me to her living room, which is just like her office: overflowing with books and journals and newspapers and magazines. I've got to move a heavy pile of books from the stained sofa before I can sit down. Miss Joe fixes me a plate of beef stew and plantain and lets me eat in the living room and asks me about my favorite class (history) and my least favorite subject (math), and when she asks me if I have a favorite novel (*Behind the Mountains* by Edwidge Danticat), she gets up right then and there to hand me books by Jamaica Kincaid and Tiphanie Yanique and stateside women too, like Zora Neale Hurston and Octavia Butler, and she tells me that these books saved her life, and I don't really know what she means by that, but I believe her when she says it.

Then she sits down across from me as one adult might sit down across from another, her legs crossed, her back straight, her hands folded in her lap. "So, Miss Murphy," she says, "what would you like to know about your mother?"

I know I can't ask her the first questions that jump to the tip of my tongue: *Where is she? Why did she leave me behind? Does she still love me?*

Instead, I ask, "How do you know my ma?"

Miss Joe lets out a laugh I'm not expecting, one so loud that it makes me jump in my seat. For a second,

I think she's laughing at me, but then I realize that she's laughing because she can't contain the joy that spreads through her. Watching that joy is like watching a piece of paper catch fire. It's like she might as well be sitting with my mother again, and they're laughing together over a joke, the funniest thing either of them had heard all year, though I get the feeling they heard something that funny every single day. Miss Joe stares at the ceiling brightly, filled to the brim with memories. "We were the closest friends. Miss Doreen Hendricks, yes, and me, Miss Loretta Joseph. We would pretend we were twins, even though we looked nothing alike, and we had our own secret language that no one was allowed to know but us, and we read books together, side by side, and as we read, we would decide that we were Janie and Pheoby, Anne and Diana, Elizabeth and Charlotte. I always let her be the star, while I was the star's best friend."

I don't know any of these people, but Miss Joe seems not to notice, because she keeps talking.

"You couldn't find one of us without the other. We even said we would marry each other," she says. "This house you sit in now was my mother's house at the time, and we decided that your mother would come here to live with me once we were finished with school. Then your mother met your father, and time got in between us, and we were not as close as friends as we once were, though we would still speak on the phone on each other's birthdays and on Christmas each year—for hours and hours, and it'd be like not a day had passed."

I have a surge of anger toward my dad. I bite my lip to keep my anger to myself, but I don't have to say anything—Miss Joe seems to see what I'm feeling. "No, this wasn't your father's fault," she says. "You'll see. Sometimes, friendships don't last, and it's not anyone's fault in particular. That's just the way it is."

Miss Joe holds her hands together. "I know that you would like to see your mother again, Miss Murphy," Miss Joe says, "and I know that it must be difficult to be without her—but I also know that she wouldn't have left without a reason."

I want to ask Miss Joe what reason my mother could possibly have—and ask how Miss Joe could possibly know—but instead, I frown at the dirty plate sitting in my lap, my head bowed, saying nothing at all. The most burning question I have is why Miss Joe would want to tell me something like that.

"I'm worried about you," she says, "and I want you to learn how to keep on going without her. Every little girl needs her mother, but sometimes that is how life is—life can't afford us everything that we want or need, so while you might not have a mother, you have a father who loves you very much, and a home and food and clothes and—" She stops herself, and she's leaning in while she's looking at me, with an expression on her face that suggests she needs nothing more than for me to understand. "Miss Murphy, you need to learn to live without her. Do you think you can do that?"

I tell her yes—of course I tell her yes, because I'm not an idiot. My dad must've spoken to Miss Joe, and together, they decided to sit me down—lie to me, get me to stop asking questions. Maybe my dad even figured out what I've been doing, that I've been planning on taking his boat, and they want me to give up on looking for my mother. There's just no way that's going to happen, because even if my dad and Miss Joe are fine with letting go of people they love, I'm not. And I never will be.

Miss Joe keeps talking to me, but my side of the conversation has long since been over, and I suppose she realizes this on her own, because it's not very much time after she takes me back to waterfront in her red pickup truck with the stack of books she's given me, and hands me ten US dollars to get back on the ferry and arrive home, where my father sits in the living room, waiting for me.

*

I know that I will somehow have to find my mother on my own. I can't ask anything else about her. I have to pretend that I'm moving on and learning to live without her, because if I don't, I know exactly what will happen: My father will be ready to lie, ready to beat back my questions. He won't have his guard down ever again. I decide then that I will never mention my mother to him—but all the while I'll continue my search in secret, and when the moment is right, I'll yank the truth right out of him.

In the morning, after he's gone to work but before I've gone to school, I open his yellowing and splintering bedroom door. There's nothing at all special about the door itself, except that it has been the same door to this bedroom for all the time this house has existed, which has existed since the slaves, which makes me realize that I'm touching a very old door. The room this door leads to was once my mom's bedroom too. The last time I stepped over the threshold was over a year ago. I never had any reason to come into this room unless it was to follow my mother inside and sit on the edge of her bed to watch her comb her hair, and put on her jewelry, and curl up beside her as she read to me. Stepping inside now sends a spike of pain through my heart, and I freeze for a moment, my hand sweating on the doorknob.

Nothing has changed. My mom's dish of tangled jewelry is still on her dresser, and her glass perfume bottles are still lined up. I can see her dresses are still hanging in the closet, like little ghosts of her missing her body, and her shoes are still lined up beneath them. Seeing her clothes and shoes sends a jolt through me. Why wouldn't she have taken them with her on her trip around the world? Only a dead woman would not need her clothes or shoes, and suddenly my mind begins to wrap around other possibilities: my dad and Miss Joe buying postcards, faking my mother's handwriting, mailing them just so I can open them and believe she really is still alive.

Heart pounding, I walk farther into the bedroom. If she's still alive, there must be proof somewhere—and if she isn't dead, then she has to be living somewhere too, somewhere I can find her. She would never turn me away. She would wrap her arms around me and apologize for leaving, and whatever reason she had—it wouldn't matter, because I'd be with her again.

I open the closest drawer, then open the next and the next, and throw open boxes piled up in the closet, and tear through jeans and folded shirts, looking for paper that has my mother's name on something, *anything*—when the front door slams open and shut. I hear heavy footsteps.

"Caroline," my father calls out, "are you still here? I forgot to leave money for the ferry."

I'm too afraid to move, so when he stops in his doorway, my dad looks down at me the way a cat might look at a mouse that has begun to eat from the kitty dish. When this was my mother's room as well, I was allowed inside at any time—but when it became only my father's room, I knew that I wasn't welcome. "Caroline," he says quietly, "what're you doing?"

I swallow and stand from where I'd been kneeling on the hard floor.

"Caroline," he says again, "what are you doing?" Except he says a rude word here too, and while my dad makes me so angry I can cry, that's one thing he's never done. He's never cursed at me.

I take a breath. I can't tell him the truth, because he can't know I'm still looking for my mother. A lie tumbles out of my mouth instead. "I was looking for money," I tell him, "to take Mister Lochana's speedboat."

Understanding crosses my dad's eyes, but a moment later, suspicion strays across it too. If he doesn't believe me, though, he doesn't say anything about it. "Well, then," he says, "I have the money here. Come on, come on."

I follow him out the door, and he snaps it shut firmly behind me.

CHAPTER
5

Miss Joe invites me to eat lunch with her inside her office, but I will never sit with a woman who wants me to be content with staying a half orphan, and besides that, I also hate the idea of Kalinda or Anise or Marie Antoinette seeing me eating in her office, because truth be told, I can't think of a single thing more pathetic than someone so lonely that they must be invited to eat with their principal, and while I really am the loneliest girl at the school, I also have my pride.

Kalinda Francis sits with Anise and Marie Antoinette every day for one week, and for one week every day I sit in the corner and watch as everyone gathers around the table, peasants begging for scraps from the queens. Except now, it's not clear who the queen is anymore. Is it Anise, sitting tall like always, yelling at anyone who gets too close? No, I think it's obvious to everyone that it's now Kalinda, who never laughs loud like the others around her but always has a special smile for everyone—a smile made and catered for each different person, the way fingerprints are different for all of us. For Anise, it's a smile that barely turns up the corners of her lips so it's more like a blank stare. For Marie Antoinette, it's a big smile that shows all her white teeth. For me, she gives a close-mouthed secretive smile, like she means for me to find her one day after school and ask her what it is she wants to tell me. Maybe she does. She looks up at me and smiles, then looks away again—but something catches her eye.

I turn my head to see what she's looking at—and there, in the corner of the cafeteria, stands a white woman in her nightgown, looking at Kalinda. She's gone before my gaze can even settle on her, and I would think it was just my mind playing tricks—but when I turn to look at Kalinda, she's watching me again—squinting her eyes, confused, but still smiling.

*

I start to make eye contact with her everywhere—in the halls, in class whenever she turns around and feels my eyes on her, even through the crowds of curly heads in the cafeteria. She never seems upset to catch me staring. She only ever has the same secretive smile. And now there's a question there, a question she has for me. It's probably the same thing I want to know from her.

Can you see the things that no one else can see too?

I could ask her. I could walk right up to her and ask if she really did—if she saw the spirit of that woman. But I'd have to ask this in front of Anise and Marie Antoinette, and if I'm wrong, and Kalinda only screws up her face at me in confusion, I know I'll never hear the end of it. Anise would never let anyone forget how Caroline Murphy is as crazy as she is evil, and there's not much else worse in the world than a crazy, evil girl. Any chance I'd have of speaking to Kalinda ever again would be wiped clean from existence.

But I *have* to know. All my life, I've seen the things no one else can see. And if someone else can see them too . . . then maybe I'm not so alone after all. The idea of not being alone—of having someone who sees me, same way I see the things that no one else can see, makes me feel like I'm real. Like I deserve to exist on this planet alongside everyone else. That I get to be here because there's someone else who wants me here too. It's the difference of being invited directly to a birthday party instead of someone being forced to hand me an invitation, same way Anise Fowler was once forced to give me an invitation to her party but whispered that if I actually came, no one would really want me there.

If Kalinda Francis can see the things no one else can see, then I *need* to know.

I decide to take a risk.

The bell for lunch rings, and Missus Wilhelmina slowly finishes her sentence, to remind us that we aren't allowed to leave until she dismisses us from class herself. Finally she does, and we all leap from our desks, and I see Kalinda moving with Anise and Marie Antoinette toward the door.

I jump in their path. There's a crowd lined up behind them, twisting and turning their heads and sucking their teeth, waiting to leave. I realize I shouldn't have stepped in front of them—should've waited until we were out in the courtyard until I could try to get Kalinda alone and away from her new friends—but I know I might never find the courage to speak to her again.

"What do you want?" Anise snaps. "Move out the way!"

I don't. I still look at Kalinda, who seems surprised—but she still gives me my smile.

"Miss Francis," I say, and immediately feel silly for using her last name. I almost do it—almost force the question out. *Can you see the things too?* But the words freeze in my throat. I swallow them and ask instead, "Would you like to join me for lunch today?"

The way Anise's eyes bug from her face would be funny if it weren't for the silence that follows. Anise recovers quickly, though, as do the people waiting behind her. There are the gasps and whispers, and Anise finally lets out a screeching laugh.

"Who does she think she is?" she demands. She begins to push past me, but stops when Kalinda says yes.

I must look like I didn't really hear her, because she says it again. "Yes. I would love to, Miss Murphy."

Stunned. We're all stunned, and Anise looks like

Kalinda turned and slapped her across the face. I let out a small laugh of disbelief.

Kalinda then takes my arm and acts like we're the oldest of friends, sweeping me away from the room, and she wastes no time at all. I had no idea anyone could have so much to say, and so quickly.

"I've only been here a week. Not just at this school, but on Saint Thomas too. I'm from Barbados, you know, and my father brought me here to live with his sister because he was having a hard time finding a job in his profession, which is carpentry. Not just fixing cabinets and that kind of thing, you know, but carving whole chairs and tables and chests and anything else imaginable from wood. He's really good at it too, but there are already so many good carpenters in Barbados that no one ever really needed him. But that's all to say that even though I've only been here for a week, I already feel at home. I almost feel like I've never lived anywhere else at all."

On and on she goes, and though this would normally be so frustrating, to listen to someone talk as much as the frogs make noise at night, I realize I don't actually mind. That I love it, in fact. She isn't making noise for the sake of making noise. She's letting me inside her head, and for the first time in my life, I feel I can almost imagine it—what it'd be like to exist as a completely different person, to have their thoughts and feelings instead of my own. It's a complete relief, like walking into my home and kicking off my loafers and sinking into the soft sofa after a very long and hot and tiring day.

We sit at the spot in the cafeteria where I normally sit alone, and I realize that though everyone usually looks at Anise's table with admiration, today all the heads have turned to us instead. They don't look at us in admiration, though. They look at us in complete shock. Some even seem angry. Like I've personally done something to offend them.

The angry stares I'm used to. I feel like I've never received any other sort of stare my entire life, except when my mother or my father looked my way. But I'm worried about Kalinda. She can't be used to such negative attention—can she?

She doesn't seem to notice, and maybe she really doesn't, since she isn't looking at anything or anyone but me. She asks me questions. She asks so many questions my head begins to spin. I've hardly finished giving one answer before she asks another, without pause or hesitation. Her questions remind me of one of those school games we used to play, when each team has to ask and answer as many questions as possible in the allotted time, and whoever has the most correct answers wins.

"You don't live on Saint Thomas?"

"No. I live on Water Island."

"But then how do you get to school?"

"There's a speedboat I take every morning with a man named Mister Lochana."

"Isn't a trip across the ocean every morning tiring?"

"It can be, yes."

"Does it feel like your heart is split between two homes? Between Saint Thomas and Water Island, I mean?"

I have to stop to think about this one, because I realize then that I don't think of either Saint Thomas or Water Island as home. How can I? My mother isn't on either island. I'm not expecting to think this, and before I know it, I can feel my eyes begin to sting and my vision become blurry as water leaks from my eyelashes. Kalinda sees, and most would be embarrassed to watch someone they don't know so well begin to cry, and even I have to say that I probably would've looked away and pretended I didn't notice, but Kalinda only grabs a napkin from her food tray and holds it out to me. She doesn't ask another question. Only looks at me and waits for me to speak. But how do I begin to explain something like this? Having a mother that's left me behind? Would Kalinda begin to accuse my mother of being a bad woman, the same way Anise does? Would Kalinda think I'd done something to deserve being deserted?

She sees that I don't want to talk about it. She smiles, but the smile has changed. It's not secretive anymore. It's knowing. I think she likes what she knows.

I decide. Now is the time to ask. With my eyes still stinging and my nose all clogged, I say in a low voice, "Did you see her too?"

She turns her head to the side and squints her eyes. "What do you mean? See who?"

I stare at her. She just keeps watching and waiting and smiling.

And I don't believe her. She's smiling at me like she's playing a game, and I don't believe her. I know she saw that white woman too.

*

That day after school, Kalinda tells me she would like to show me her house, and even though Mister Lochana is usually waiting for me in the hot sun by waterfront as soon as the school day ends, I agree. We walk through Main Street, which only the oldest of old folks call Dronningen's Gade. There's a traffic jam longer than a slithering python, and I have to look where I'm going, because it's easy to twist my foot on the broken cobblestone road. Tourists smelling like sweat and sunscreen swarm the street, standing desperately under the ice-cold air-conditioning of the jewelry stores.

Usually, I hate this walk more than anything else. Too many tourists to dodge and too many blaring horns and too much heat beating down from the blazing sun with absolutely no shade. But with Kalinda, it becomes a walk I could happily take every day for the rest of my life. I can barely get over the excitement, the thrill, of having someone walk beside me willingly with a smile on their face, speaking to me as one friend might speak to another. Is it too soon to consider Kalinda a friend? I hope it isn't too soon at all—that maybe she's even begun to consider me a friend too.

We reach the end of the crowded lane and walk to where the old market used to be.

"Do you see that man there?" she asks. I turn to look, but there are too many men sitting under the shade of a mahogany tree. "That man is Mister Thompson, and he lives in my neighborhood and plays an accordion and sings into all hours of the night. He makes my auntie cuss rotten because he keeps her up, but I like to sit outside on the front steps and listen to him until I fall asleep right there on the concrete, but I have to wake up before my auntie or my dad does, so they'll never know I left my bed."

"Why would you want to leave your bed to listen to that man play the accordion?" I ask, but then immediately regret it. Would she think I was being rude or mean? I have a way of asking things, a way of speaking—"combative," Miss Joe calls it—because I always automatically assume everyone just wants to be in a fight with me, seeing that, so far in my life, most people have.

But Kalinda doesn't seem offended at all. She shrugs. "Have you ever heard an accordion play?"

"No, I haven't."

"They're not the prettiest instruments to listen to," she says, "but I don't like that there are some instruments that are considered prettier than others. I feel like those instruments are always listened to. Like the guitar or the piano. But it isn't fair that they should be listened to all the time, only because someone has decided they're prettier. The accordion has just as much sound. It's different than the other instruments. I like that it's different. That's what makes it important."

I can't stop staring at her. "I think I might be the accordion."

She laughs long and hard.

I can't help but feel ashamed. I think she's laughing at me. "Why's that funny?"

"I'm sorry," she says. "I'm only laughing because— well, I think I'm the accordion too," she says.

I still don't see why this is funny—and I don't think she could be any further from an accordion. "You're not an accordion," I tell her. "You're something else entirely. You're—you're the violin," I say decidedly.

Her smile fades away. "Violins are so sad. I'd hate to be a violin."

Yet I know with absolute certainty that this is exactly the instrument that should be used to describe Kalinda.

"And you're not an accordion," she tells me. "You're a drum."

She watches me, waiting for my response, but I have no words—I only know suddenly that I want to take her hand, and so I do. I take her hand with my sweaty palm, and her fingers feel burning hot in my own, like she has a fever, and she immediately tugs her hand away from mine, surprised. I'm surprised too, that she wouldn't let me keep her hand in mine—and I feel the shame even hotter than the sun—but Kalinda doesn't say anything about it. She instead points behind me to a store, and we walk into the fresh, air-conditioned store that sells seashells for earrings and thin tie-dyed dresses that make me feel like I'm under the sea with all the swirling colors of fish and coral and clear blue water and seaweed.

"Do you like any of these earrings?" she asks me.

I don't actually like jewelry very much, but I'm

afraid to tell her this, especially after she's taken her hand from mine. Will she think I'm strange, that I'm a girl who doesn't like jewelry? Maybe, since she's said she likes accordions, she won't mind.

"Which one is your favorite?"

I hesitate. "I don't like earrings very much."

She seems surprised. "I've never met someone who doesn't like earrings. But I think that's okay. Do you like any of these shells?"

I point out one shell that is flat and has waves and looks like a fan, with a soft pink underbelly where a pearl might have once been found. "I can't buy this for you," Kalinda says, "but I'll try to find a shell that's even better than this one."

This will be the second gift I've ever received from someone who is not my mother or my father. I think it might be a gift of pity, because she knows I have no other friends. I know immediately I want to give something to her too, though I have no idea what. I decide I've never had such a good time before in my life, but then I feel guilty for thinking something like that, after all the good times I'd spent with my mother.

Just as we're walking, I see two women holding hands. It's the first time I've ever seen two women holding hands like that. Girls my age, like Kalinda and me, hold hands all the time to show that they care for each other. (I realize with a pang that perhaps Kalinda didn't want to hold my hand because she doesn't care for me at all.) But grown women, even older than Miss Joe and Missus Wilhelmina and my mom? I've never seen anything like that before.

The two women are both white tourists and old, with sagging skin and too-short shorts showing off their blue veins. People turn their heads to stare, but those two women don't seem to mind at all. They just keep on walking and holding hands and smiling at one another.

Kalinda sees them holding hands. "Disgusting," she says. "They can't see they're both women?" She laughs. "Does one of them think that she's a man?" She laughs again.

My heart falls. I don't know why it would. Maybe because I would like to hold Kalinda's hand too, and I know now that we never will—not in the way these two women do. I'd thought, since she'd said everything she did about Mister Thompson and his accordion...but maybe that was a silly thing to think.

I make myself laugh. "How can they not? I can see they're women, just by standing all the way over here. How can they not know they're women?"

But Kalinda's past laughing now. "I think it's gross. It's wrong." She says it loudly, just as we pass the two old women still holding each other's hands, as they pause to look at jewelry in a window. One woman hears and looks at me and Kalinda with a frown, but not the sort of frown Missus Wilhelmina has for me when I'm in trouble—but the saddest frown I've seen from an adult. Like she might begin to cry right then and there.

She's still looking at us when I tell Kalinda, "I agree."

Kalinda gives me a smile that warms my chest, but I look back to the older white woman and have to look away again, because I see she's even closer to crying now, and a part of me would like to join her.

*

Kalinda's house is past Main Street and beside a large cemetery. Whitewashed cement blocks carrying the dead are stacked on top of one another, building a graveyard city that's bleached like bones in the sun. We pass the children's grave with the overflowing brown and crispy flowers, fluttering in the wind like cockroach wings. I keep my hands behind my back, since the ghosts of children have been known to bite off fingers, or so I've been told.

Kalinda tells me a story. "When I was six years old, I watched a girl die. We were in church, and she collapsed in the pew, and her father held her and her mother screamed and a man who had once studied medicine rushed to her, but before he even reached her, it was too late. That was the day I stopped being a child," she says. "Adults—my parents, my teachers—they look at me and see a little girl who knows nothing about life and death, someone they need to protect . . . but now that I've seen death with my own eyes, they have nothing to protect me from anymore."

When I look at her, for a moment it feels like I might as well be looking at a mirror, and not even that, because I feel like I know her more than I even know myself.

"There was once a man that lived on top of the hill on Water Island," I tell her. "He died in a fire, after fireworks exploded above him. When I learned he died, I stopped being a child too."

Kalinda nods at me, agreeing that neither of us are really children anymore. We're not adults either, because adults have forgotten how to live, and I know Kalinda and I have not. Adults wouldn't understand something like this—that Kalinda and I are neither children nor adults. They only look at us and see two twelve-year-old girls, and so think we know nothing about life or death. They assume we have nothing but innocence. I think we must be closer to being alive than adults. They've been alive too long to remember the passion of life. And Kalinda and I, maybe we've been alive too long too, and the only animals on this Earth that really understand life are the insects that are born and mate and die within seconds. They're really the ones that understand it all.

As we walk, I realize there are now two things that Kalinda and I have in common: the reality that we are no longer children, and the fact that we can both see the things no one else can see.

I want to ask her again. I want to ask her for the truth this time, and tell her that I know she's lying, and demand to know why she's lying about this, when it's so clear that we both looked up in the cafeteria, both looked in that woman's direction, and for a split second, Kalinda had fear in her eyes, because she had een something no one else could see.

But what if it isn't true? What if it's my own mind playing games with me, and not Kalinda? What if she's not lying at all, and she really didn't see anyone there, and she would have no idea what I was talking about if I dared to ask her? I'd make such a fool of myself, and I'm already lucky enough as it is, that Kalinda decided to speak with me and walk with me and invite me to her home. It's the first time I've ever been to a classmate's house before. If I insist that we speak about this again and again—well, I don't know how Kalinda will react. Tomorrow I might find myself sitting alone in the cafeteria.

No. Best to keep silent about this.

We come to her house, which is in a neighborhood where men slam dominoes on a rickety table under the shade of a yellow mango tree, and where the roads are lined with rusting cars missing their tires. Her concrete house is missing its paint, or maybe it's just been that long since anyone painted its walls.

The inside is missing its furniture as well, except for a single chair and a little table that doesn't even reach my knees. Halls break away from the room, which is where all the furniture must be. There's a man who I think must be Kalinda's father sitting in the living room, which doesn't have a TV, and he's bent over an ornate chair leg growing from the block of wood that stands on a square of plastic and wood shavings.

He sees us, and we say good afternoon, and so does he, but then he goes back to his carving, and I wonder why he doesn't ask me for my name or say that it's nice to meet one of Kalinda's friends. Does Kalinda bring new friends to the house so often? I feel a pinch of jealousy. But then Kalinda does something with her hands so it looks like she's pointing and then twisting her fingers, and he nods again, and Kalinda smiles and walks on down the hall to where her bedroom must be. Every door we pass on the way is closed, until we reach the door at the end of the hall. Kalinda pushes it open, and I see that her mattress is on the floor, but she has the most beautiful dressing table, and her nightstand looks like it's made from gold. Kalinda sits on the edge of her mattress and tells me her father hasn't built her bed frame yet, though it's next on his list.

"He makes beautiful furniture."

"I'll tell him you said that."

We sit in silence for some time. I try to think long and hard about what to say to Kalinda. I don't want to tell her how excited I am, how overjoyed, that she's chosen to be my friend, to the point that I would like to hold her hand in the same way the two white women walking down the street did, because then I think Kalinda wouldn't speak to me anymore. But then I'm not really sure what else to say, because it feels like there's nothing that can be said until she understands how I feel about her at this very moment.

"He can't hear," Kalinda says.

I'm confused. "Who can't hear?"

"My father," she says, before she launches into a story of how her father's greatest dream had once been to be the best guitarist of Barbados, playing in his local band and singing soca and calypso, but when he was eighteen his disease near took his life and succeeded in taking all his hearing, so he had no choice but to find a new dream. "That seems like a most difficult thing to do. Finding a dream alone is hard. I've spent many days wondering what my own dream should be. But I'm not sure I have any dreams yet. Maybe my dream is to find a dream. Find something to live for. Can you imagine, doing all that work to find something to live for, and then being forced to find another dream at the end of it all?"

This is such an interesting thing to say that I'm intimidated into silence. Kalinda intimidates me. Maybe I was wrong. Maybe I really am still just a child, while Kalinda is the only one who isn't a child anymore. It's enough to make me wonder if Kalinda is even really from the same mundane world I was born in.

She smiles at me. "Do you have any dreams, Caroline?"

I might as well be mute, like Marie Antoinette and the Chief, because I don't say anything for a long time, and I can't think of anything to say for as long a time either, but Kalinda doesn't speak and doesn't look like she plans on speaking until I give her an answer. At first this is even more nerve-racking than if she'd been watching me impatiently, wondering whether she'd chosen a fool for her newest friend—but then her open stare and knowing smile lets me see that she doesn't mind at all, and she'd be happy sitting with me for the rest of the afternoon in silence, if that's what I chose to do.

"My mother," I finally say. The words come from my mouth without me even thinking of this as the answer. "I want to find my mother."

She seems a little surprised. Her smile fades away and she sits straighter, her ankles crossed and her hands folded in her lap, like she's sitting in church. "Where did your mother go?" she asks, so quietly she might as well be whispering.

The words are too painful to say aloud. I feel a burning in my throat. I'm too ashamed to look Kalinda in the eye.

She puts her hand on top of mine. It's still warm. I know she doesn't mean to take my hand in the same way the two women earlier did, but it's still comforting, after she'd yanked her hand away from mine before.

"You don't have to be afraid to tell me," Kalinda tells me. "You could admit that you were sent to hell and you escaped, and I wouldn't have any judgment toward you."

I believe her. I'm still afraid, though, because I think I might have more than enough judgment for myself. It feels like I've done something so horrible that my own mom had to get up and leave me. I take a breath and speak the words: "One year and three months ago, my mother left home."

Kalinda is nodding, her hand still on top of mine. "Why did she leave?"

I shake my head. My eyes are starting to sting with salt water. The ocean is made of salt water, and I wonder for a moment if it's possible that we were actually born of the sea and crawled ourselves onto these islands.

"I don't know why she left," I say. "I think it's possible that she doesn't love me anymore, and so she felt she had to go."

Kalinda seems to listen with all her heart, eyes shining bright. "I don't see how that could be possible at all," she says. "There isn't anything about you that would make me feel that you aren't someone to love."

She takes her hand away, and barely gives my heart a moment to stop beating before she says, "My mother stayed in Barbados as well. When s̶ told me she was staying, months befor̶e̶ w̶ d to leave, I thought that̶ either. And I'm still afraid ̶t̶h̶i̶s̶ ̶i̶s̶ ̶t̶r̶u̶e̶, sometimes. She says that it's because we can't all afford to go, and so my brothers and sisters stayed with her, while I'm here with my father. I still wonder if she chose to send me away because she doesn't love me."

"That's not possible," I tell her. "It's impossible not to love someone like you."

She laughs. "Thank you, Caroline."

She smiles and jiggles her feet as she looks at me. "Even though I've only known you for one day, I now think of you as my friend," Kalinda tells me. "I don't choose my friends easily." She uses her adult voice, so I know that she's very serious.

I don't tell her that this means more to me than anything anyone has ever told me, because she's now the first friend I've ever had who wasn't my mother, and the only friend I've ever had since my mother left me.

That would be too embarrassing to admit. So instead I tell her, "You're my friend now too."

"Are you still looking for her?" she asks. "Your mother, I mean."

I'm always looking for her. Walking down the road, every woman I see with honey-brown skin makes my heart beat harder and my throat close up so I can't swallow, can't breathe—and then the woman turns around and I see it's not my ma at all, and I could cry from disappointment.

"No." I didn't plan to lie, but that's what I do anyway. "No," I say again, "I'm not still looking for her." Maybe it's only fair that I've lied, since Kalinda won't tell me the truth about the things no one else can see. Now we're even.

Though I'm not sure I want us to be.

*

I can always feel the woman in black near. A shadow going in and out, like a candle's flame flickering in the breeze. It's impossible, isn't it? But I always feel her there, watching me. Who is she? And what does she want to tell me? Because that's one thing I'm sure of. She's trying to let me know something.

The woman in black is waiting for me when I get home. Even though I'd had one of the best afternoons of my life at Kalinda's house, I can already start to feel the whispers inside my mind, questioning if I really love my mom at all, if I can so easily forget about her for the promise of a new friend. I begin to question if I deserve my mother's love, if I can so easily treat her this way, so easily forget all about her. And so I begin to question if I even really deserve to be loved at all—and if I don't deserve to be loved, then perhaps I don't deserve to be alive.

I don't think adults expect that anyone who is twelve years old and shouldn't have any worries in this world can think about something like that, but I wonder about it all the time. I'm wondering it as I walk into my bedroom.

She's standing there in the corner of my room, and she's not leaving this time, even when I look at her directly in the eye. She watches me without an expression on her face, because it seems even that is shrouded in blackness, in shadow, in darkness that's growing and spreading across my wall and my bed until it seems like it's night even though I know full well it's day, and I can't see anything at all but the glint of the white in her eye, almost as though her eyes are glowing themselves, stars shining in the night sky.

I can't speak for a long time. Fear has gripped my throat. But finally I manage to force out "Who are you?"

She stands there in the corner of my room.

"What do you want?"

She still only stands.

"I'm not a person to harass," I spit out with fake bravery. As soon as I say it, I flinch back. I decide then and there that she's not my mother, because if she were my mother, she would've come to me a long time ago, wrapping her arms around me, and I wouldn't even care that she's shrouded in shadow, because she would be my mother. This woman—she's too cold to even look at fully, too distant, not even a stranger, because with a stranger at least you can feel you'll eventually become friends, but with this woman I know that will never happen.

And I realize then and there that something else is just as clear: The woman in black is the reason my mother has disappeared.

"Did you take her?" I ask, my voice such a whisper that even I barely hear it.

She's gone. Gone like she'd never even been there at all. Light reaches the corner of my room again, and the room fills with yellow. I stand where I am for a long time, wondering if she was only a part of my imagination, if she's only been a trick of the light, creating shadows in the corner of my room in the form of a woman standing there, watching me.

Maybe I'm just crazy, crazier than the man that spits at tourists by the docks. Just as crazy as I'm afraid I've always been.

But if she's real—if the woman in black exists as much as I do standing right here on my own two feet—then I also know she has something to do with it. With everything. She knows something about my mom. I'm going to get her back.

CHAPTER

6

I don't know for sure if the woman in black has my mom, but I do know that the woman in black has something to do with my mother's disappearance. It can't be a coincidence that she has continued to appear in my life, coming to me that much more frequently since my mother left, as if laughing at me—taunting me. Maybe she knows where my mother is. To find my mom, I have to find the woman in black first.

I'm not sure what makes her come sometimes and leave others. She has to have a reason for her ways, but whatever those reasons are, I don't know them at all.

I do know one thing, though: I've never actually tried to call to the woman in black. I've never asked her to suddenly appear and scare half my life away. It's never been something that's occurred to me that I could try. Is

it even possible to call her—to make her come, to per-
ha_ about my
mothe_ _ _ _ _ _ _ _ _ _ _ _ _ _ _ _ _ _ _de and my
mother stumbles out from the darkness?

I don't know the answer to that, but I think I know
where I might find one.

My school has a library that used to be a classroom,
with wooden and plastic shelves covering the walls all
around the room, with every single book imaginable,
since all the books are ones that have been donated from
anyone and everyone all over the island. Hardly anyone
ever goes inside, because the ones who do go inside are
declared to be the strangest of misfits that no one is ever
allowed to like anymore, but since I'm disliked by everyone anyway (well, except Kalinda now), I've always found
it easy to stroll inside and spend time with myself and the
hundreds of worlds lined up before me. I've learned endless things in this library, even things my mother would
not have thought to teach me, such as the fact that there's
an entire town filled with rotting dolls near Mexico City,
or that there's a fungi that takes over the brains of ants and
makes those ants do their bidding, and the fact that there

could be an infinite number of universes, which means that there could be an infinite number of Caroline Murphys living on an infinite number of Water Islands— except that maybe some of those Caroline Murphys aren't on Water Island at all. There's an infinite number of possibilities and outcomes for each of those universes, so maybe my mother met my father while he was still living abroad, and they got married and had me while they were living in Paris. I could be speaking French in another universe. I could be happy and normal and popular, as popular as Anise Fowler. I could be in love with a boy, like all the other girls in my class. Or maybe my mother has not met my father at all in another universe, and so I don't even exist. Maybe this is the only universe where I am here, and this is me, and there's only one universe where there's a Caroline Murphy.

I love the library, and I've spent many of my afternoons there, so I think it's possible that the answers I need—everything I need to know about the woman in black—can be found here. I walk into the shadowed and empty and hot library classroom, which smells like spilled milk and mothballs, and I look for books about ghosts and spirits first, since I think this is most likely what the woman in black is, and then I look up demons in the Caribbean next, since this is, I think, another possibility.

I carry the stack of books to a table at the very back of the room, and the librarian stares at me suspiciously from her desk.

I learn more than I would ever like to learn about ghosts and spirits and demons. Enough to know that I'll certainly have nightmares tonight, and maybe even nightmares for the rest of my life. I learn that the Caribbean is a place where spirits and ghosts exist more than anywhere else in the world—that the air is so full of spirits that I'm breathing them in, right now as I read.

I also learn that there are some who feel ghosts and spirits and demons do not exist but are made up completely in one's own mind, and especially in the minds of those who are delusional and have been through emotional traumas to help them cope, which makes me fear that the woman in black isn't real at all, and is only something I've made up in my own head—perhaps something to desperately explain the disappearance of my mother.

The woman in black—not real. It was something I'd

only wondered before, but now the possibility of this truth sears through me. Her existence reminds me of when I think of something so outlandish and silly, such as the desire to hold Kalinda's hand, and I think of saying this outlandish thing out loud, I realize how ridiculous the thought is. Yes—it's entirely possible that the woman in black isn't real, and the things that no one else can see aren't real, and I've simply lied to myself to feel special, and to explain why my mother would have left me, when it's clear that she left because she simply doesn't love me.

I slam the book shut so loud that I hear the librarian clear her throat behind me. This is one possibility that I can't ignore. But what if I'm wrong? What if the woman in black does exist and she knows something about the reason my mother is gone?

I continue reading, keep skimming, until I look at the clock and see that I have mere seconds to learn about the woman in black before the bell rings and I have to return to class, until finally in the very last book, in the very last chapter, I do learn one useful thing: a way to communicate with a ghost.

It's a story about a man whose daughter had

unexpectedly died sleeping in her bed one night, and so the man decided to call upon her to say good-bye. It's just about the saddest story I've ever read, and I have to wipe my eyes quickly so the librarian doesn't ask me why I'm crying. The book tells me about how this man managed to speak to his child again, and I know that this is what I'll have to try if I want to speak to the woman in black. Unfortunately, the text also specifically says not to use this trick on a demon, for the demon will surely overpower and possess or even kill you. Which is a horrifying thing to read, for while I don't know if the woman in black really exists, I'm also not really sure whether the woman in black would be a spirit or a ghost or a demon if it turns out that she's as real as I am.

This is something I'll have to figure out—and there's really only one way to do that.

The bell rings. I tuck this one book into my schoolbag, as I've done with many other books before, and hurry out of the library before the librarian's suspicious stare burns a hole right through the back of my head.

When I'm finally home, I close and lock my door and take my book and flip it open so it's like a bird resting in my hand. The instructions from the man's story are clear: I have to light a candle and speak the woman in black's name. I don't know her name, so I will call her "woman in black." I then have to pray to her until she finally appears. This book says that some people have a stronger ability to call spirits and demons forward than others, but I figure I must have a strong ability, else she wouldn't appear to me in the first place. (Unless, of course, the only reason she appears to me is because I've made her up in my head.) Once she comes, she won't be able to leave, because I'll have poured a ring of salt that she will find impenetrable, and she'll have no choice but to stay and speak with me.

I tell myself I'm not afraid, because I'm prepared: The candle is lit, the lights off, the salt poured—but of course my heart is hammering in my chest so hard that it's a painful beat.

I call for her. "Woman in black," I say, but I'm not really sure what to say after that. "Woman in black," I say again, my voice not quite as shaky as it was the first time.

I sit there for what feels like at least ten minutes, legs crossed and cramping, but when I look at the clock again, only one minute has passed. So I sit there for ten minutes, which truly feels like an hour, periodically calling for her again and again—but I have a feeling she's not coming. And I can't ignore the obvious explanation for why she won't be coming to visit me. It looks like little Caroline Murphy really is as crazy as she is evil.

What should I do? Carry salt with me wherever I go so I can throw it at her and trap her and question her about my mother? Someone would notice the salt, surely, and it'd be yet another reason why Caroline Murphy should not be allowed to have any friends.

But I do have one friend. Kalinda. She has seen the woman in the courtyard—she can see the things no one else can see.

Maybe she could help me trap the woman in black. She could help me find my mother.

*

Kalinda. Kalinda. Kalinda. It's like a song stuck in my head. I can't think of anything else. She competes for my thoughts. Sometimes she wins. Kalinda Francis. Kalinda Francis. Kalinda Francis.

She catches me staring at her all the time, but she never seems to mind. Just keeps smiling like there's nothing strange about it, nothing strange at all, that she would catch me watching her. I try to stop, but I can't. One look at her sends my heart beating and bouncing against the walls in my chest, and sometimes it feels like it gets lodged in my throat too, and even though it feels like we've known each other since the moment we both came out of our mothers' wombs, I look at her and I can't speak a word.

We sit in her bedroom. I love her bedroom now even more than I love my own. I love seeing her, her dark skin the kind of brown that can't be found anywhere else in nature, only on her, and I love seeing her twisted locks piled up onto her head. I love being near her. Love how she always smells like lemongrass, especially in the early mornings, yellow warmth radiating from her skin and clothes.

"Are you okay, Caroline?" she asks. She smiles.

Warmth spreads under my cheeks. "I'm okay," I tell her. I'm still trying to find the courage to ask her about the things no one else can see—and for her to help find the woman in black.

She must know I'm lying, but she seems uncon-
cerned. "I want you to close your eyes," she says.

I hesitate. "Why?"

"Don't you trust me?"

More than I even trust myself, but I'm not about to
say that out loud. So I just close my eyes, and for a second,
I hear nothing but myself breathing, the crinkling of the
bedsheets, can practically hear Kalinda's smile, and I smell
the lemongrass as she comes closer, and then around my
neck something cold bites into my skin, and I open my
eyes to see a necklace with a seashell hanging from its end.

"I made it for you," she tells me. I would've been
nervous to say such a thing, but she doesn't seem nervous
about her declaration at all. "I know you said that you
don't like jewelry, but I do, and I wanted to give you
something that I like. Do you like it?"

I haven't even really looked at it. "I love it." *I love
you.* The thought comes to me as fast as a bolt of lightning, and I've never known something to be more true. I
remember Missus Wilhelmina teaching us about stories
of children falling in love, and saying that no one so
young can really love so deeply—that we don't even know

what *love* truly is—but I know now, in this moment, that I love Kalinda Francis.

I fancy myself brave and think I'm the sort of person who will always speak my mind, but that's the one thing I'm too afraid to say. I clutch the seashell in the palm of my hand. I don't like necklaces, but I don't think I'll ever take this one off. "Thank you."

"You're welcome, Caroline."

*

Weeks pass like this, and after nearly a month of spending almost every moment with each other and not getting into fights, never tiring of each other's presence, Kalinda and I become Carolinda, we're together so much of the time. Most become used to it, watching us turn to exchange looks in class and mouth words to each other during morning prayer and hold hands together at our lunch table, since Kalinda has begun to let me take her fingers with mine, though it's clear that it isn't at all in the way that I would like to be holding hands. We only hold hands in the way that young girls do, when they're five and skipping down the street together. Most girls our age have stopped holding hands, even if they're friends, because that's something babies do, but Kalinda doesn't seem to care at all that we're twelve years old and should not be holding hands as friends. So as we sit together, that's what we do.

And I think some would've even joined us too if Kalinda and I hadn't made ourselves a little invisible shield to say we didn't want anyone near us but ourselves. Even a whole month later, Anise still looked bowled over by how everything had turned out, like Kalinda and I had taken turns spitting in her face.

And everything would be perfect too, except that I still don't have my mom, and I still don't have the courage to ask Kalinda for help with the woman in black, and I'm afraid that I'm actually insane.

But on the day that is my mother's birthday, the house smells like spoiling bottles of rum, and I remember how my mother would buy me a gift on these days too, because she would say that she wanted to celebrate the best thing that'd ever happened to her.

I need Kalinda's help. I know I have to find the courage to ask her.

I take in a deep breath, like I plan on sucking all the oxygen out of the air, and I let it out slowly again, same way God must have blown out through his mouth to create wind on the second day. "You can see it," I tell her. I fiddle with the necklace she made me. It's still cold to the touch, even so many weeks later. We're sitting on her bed, the frame her daddy built a golden brown so we might as well be sitting on a throne together.

She doesn't know what I'm talking about, but she looks at me curiously. "See what?"

"You can see the things no one else can see too."

She squints her eyes at me.

"You know." I lower my voice. "The spirits."

Then, quick as a flash, she puts her hand over my mouth. It's hot and tastes like salt. "Don't say that," she whispers, and almost sounds angry about it.

"So you can see," I say against her hand. Relief washes through me—maybe I'm not so crazy after all.

"Would you be quiet?" She doesn't say anything, so it's just the two of us looking at each other, her fingers damp against my chin. When she decides she can trust me to speak again, she lowers her hand.

"I'll only say this once, so pay attention," she whispers. "They don't like being spoken about. Speaking about the spirits is like calling their names, and once you call their names, they'll have the freedom to follow you and torture you until the end of time."

For a second, I don't talk, I'm so relieved she can see the things I can too. If she can, then I'm not crazy—unless it's just the two of us together that are. Or unless she's playing the cruelest game of all.

I finally speak. "How're we supposed to talk about them, then?" I whisper back.

"We don't." She sits straighter with a finality that I guess is supposed to be the period on our conversation, but I know I can't give up, not that easily.

"But why not?"

"I said I was only going to tell you once."

"Just because we're scared of them?" I sit straighter too, to match her straightness, and she looks surprised by it. I must admit, I'm surprised by it too. Kalinda has always been the one in charge of this relationship. The one who does not need me as much as I need her. She must have realized this, for it's a plain fact, right there for both of us to see. She doesn't take advantage of it, but in the same way that a student knows less than a teacher, I've always followed her around and listened to her thoughts and tried my best to answer her questions. I've never sat with my back as straight as hers.

"If I'm right about this," I say, "then they have my mom. And I want her back."

Kalinda takes in a big breath, like she also plans on taking all the air that exists in this world into her lungs, then stops and let's it all out again. "That's an important reason enough, I cannot lie."

I wait for her to speak again.

"Most days I still don't even know if they're real," she says. "If they're just in my head."

"Then they're just in both our heads, and we're crazy together."

"Well, I don't know if our heads are real either."

At first I don't know what she means by that, but I don't have much time to think on it anyway, because suddenly she stands from her bed and she tells me she'll consider everything I've said and will come to me tomorrow morning in the courtyard at school, and really it isn't until I'm walking out her house and down the road past the rusted cars and the men playing dominoes that I realize what she meant. She doesn't know if our heads are real either because she doesn't know if we're real either. And the idea gets me to thinking, because it's never occurred to me before, that we might not even really exist. That we're the figment of someone's imagination, some crazy person or maybe spirit or god that's just dreamed up each and every single one of us. Maybe the woman in black is real, while I'm the one who doesn't exist.

*

I wait for Kalinda in the shade of a barren mango tree in the courtyard, away from everyone else. No one has touched me or laughed at me or thrown rocks at me since Kalinda and I became Carolinda, and I know I should be grateful, but for some reason, that just makes me even angrier. They won't throw rocks at Carolinda, but they will throw rocks at Caroline? That doesn't feel very fair at all.

Kalinda comes walking, like she promised. She walks up the stairs and straight for me, and coming up on the steps behind her is the white woman in her dressing gown.

I grab Kalinda's hand. "You can see her too," I say.

"Yes," Kalinda says.

"Who is she?" I ask.

"I don't know, but she must have me mistaken for someone else. Someone she knew when she was alive. Or maybe she knows my ancestors. Or maybe I will meet her in the future."

I frown in confusion. "In the future? But she's dead—she can only be a ghost from the past."

"No," Kalinda says, "not necessarily. Time is something we've made up in our heads. Time isn't real at all. The time before I was born, and all the days that I'm alive, and the time after I will die is all one in the same, Caroline. The spirits could be friends from the future or people from our past. Who knows? Maybe a spirit I see could even be me."

I look back to the steps, and the woman has disappeared. "I'm not sure what to think about any of that," I tell Kalinda. "I don't want to think about spirits or ghosts at all. I just want to know where my mother is."

"Yes, I know. I've thought about it," she tells me, "and I will speak about them openly, but only because you need help finding your mother."

I tell her that I'm most grateful. She asks me what it is that I want to know.

I ask Kalinda, "What do you know about ghosts?"

And she says, "More than I should."

She tells me the house she lived in on Barbados, where her mother and seven other siblings currently live, was haunted, as most houses in the islands are, and she said her house had a dead little boy who liked to play too many games. He'd turn on the radio or turn up the dial on the oven so your dinner would be burned and he'd pinch your arm if you weren't paying him enough attention. And then there was the ghost that haunted the library next to her school, a ghost that took no shape at all, wasn't a man or a woman or a child, but was the overwhelming emotion of rage and fury and betrayal, and anyone who happened to walk through that emotion would come out ready to fight anyone and anything. She told me she walked through that spot one day, and she'd never been so angry before in her life.

"You're surrounded by spirits," I tell her.

"I always have been. I think it's because they know I can see them. You can see them too." When I nod, she asks, "But why do you need to know about them, to get your mother back?"

"There's one spirit in particular. I don't know; she could even be a demon. I've seen her all my life. One day, I fell off a boat, and she was waiting for me on the ocean floor. She doesn't have a name, but I call her the woman in black, and since the day my mother left, she has been appearing to me more and more. She's been following me up and down this island, and I think she must have something to do with my mother's disappearance."

Kalinda nods, listening. "It sounds like a classic haunting to me. But why is she haunting you?" she asks.

"I think that she's taken my mom. Stolen her away, hidden her somewhere."

"Why would she do something like that?"

"I don't know."

"And besides, she could have taken your mother and disappeared entirely, if it was just your mother that she wanted."

"Maybe she wants to tease and taunt me, the way that boy did in your old house." But even as I say it, I know that the woman in black would have no reason to do something like that to me. "Or maybe she knows something—maybe she wants to tell me something about my mother's disappearance."

Kalinda takes this into consideration, before she stands straighter. "I have something important to tell you, Caroline," Kalinda says. "Please listen carefully. There's a chance that this woman in black has nothing to do with your mother's disappearance at all. There's also a chance that she only wants to speak to you, like you've said, and wants to tell you where your mother can be found. And then there's the chance that she's stolen your mother away entirely. If it's the last possibility, and the woman in black took your mother, then they're in the spirit world."

"The spirit world?"

"Yes, the spirit world," Kalinda says again. "Where all the spirits go. Not very many people are taken there, but when they are, they see incredible things. Skies of flowers, and hills made of water, creatures you can't even imagine. That's what I hear. If your mom was taken by the spirits..." Kalinda starts, but doesn't seem to plan on finishing. I wait until she takes a breath and opens her mouth again. "I don't think you'll get her back again."

I don't know what to say. What do I say to that, when the thought of seeing my mother again is the only thing that's mattered—the one thing that's given me a purpose in this world? "That's a lie," I say.

"It's not a lie," Kalinda says. She doesn't look offended that I even suggested it. "Once they take you, they don't let go. You'll be trapped in the spirit world if you go there to find her."

"But it's possible to get there without the spirits taking you?"

"You didn't hear me," she says. "It'll be impossible to get out again."

"That doesn't matter," I say, and it's the truth. If I'm trapped there and my mother is trapped there too, then that just means I have my mom. Where we are doesn't matter—not coming back to Water Island or Saint Thomas doesn't matter. I can see a flinch of hurt on Kalinda's face, though, which turns into a stony anger just a split second later, and I feel guilt twisting my insides. I feel guilty, because I know that it does matter. I would miss Kalinda. I would miss my father. I would even miss Miss Joe. But I can't let that stop me. More than anyone else, I have missed my mother so much more, and it hurts how badly I want to see her again, how badly I want her to wrap her arms around me and tell me that everything will be fine, as long as we have each other.

And so I don't apologize for implying that Kalinda doesn't matter to me, because while it's true that I would miss her terribly, it's also true that I need my mother more. I ask, "How do I get to the spirit world?"

Kalinda looks ready to suck her teeth. I've never seen her so mad. But she takes a second before she says anything again. "You must remember, there's a chance that the woman in black knows where your mother is, and is only trying to tell you the truth."

"And there's also a chance that she's taken my mother." And I feel, with all my heart, that this is exactly what has happened. Or perhaps this is what I want to have happened most of all. This would explain why my mother would leave me—this would explain that she hadn't left me by choice.

I ask her again. "How do I get to the spirit world?"

"The eclipse," she says. "The solar eclipse is the only time humans can leave this world for the spirits'. That's when they become our shadows and we become theirs. You can switch with a spirit—let them into our world in your place."

I look at Kalinda, who isn't looking at me, and I want to ask her how she knows so much about this world and crossing over to be with the spirits, and spirits crossing over to ours, but then I get so scared at what her answer will be—that she knows this because this world wasn't originally hers, and that the real Kalinda is now trapped on the other side—that I decide it's best not to ask it at all.

Anyone listening to us would dismiss our conversation as child's play. They would say that our imaginations have gotten the best of us. I feel that heartbeat of reality, the idea of saying these things out loud to anyone else, and realize how outlandish this all is—how insane, how impossible.

But I'm sharing these thoughts with Kalinda. Maybe this isn't so insane after all.

"If you're serious about this," Kalinda says, "then you have to wait until the next eclipse."

"When will that be?" I ask her.

"Three months and three days," she says with a certainty that makes me wonder why she would know this, how she would know this, unless she was a regular visitor of the spirit world herself.

Three months and three days. She might as well have told me eternity.

"But this is good," she quickly adds, "because now you can have time to think about whether you really want to do this."

"I really want to do this."

"Then," she tries again, "you can have time to prepare. Make sure you're ready."

I don't know what I have to prepare for in the spirit world, but I already know I'm ready. I've been ready to see my mother again since the last time I saw her, before that morning when I woke up and couldn't find her, that night which didn't seem special at all, where she was sitting in the living room with her feet up on the center table, reading a book that I can't even remember the title of, with me sitting next to her, stretching my feet out to rest them on the table too, even though my legs were too short for me to sit comfortably.

"I'm ready" is all I say on that. Kalinda must believe me, because she only nods.

*

As I walk home, I think more about Kalinda's anger. I would be angry too if she told me she was leaving this world for another that may or may not exist, so flippantly and easily, like I didn't really matter to her at all. Of course she matters to me. She's the first friend I've ever had. The one person who's made me feel like I deserve to be alive. I love her.

I decide that since she's helping me find my mom, I should at least tell her the truth. She deserves to know that she's loved by someone. It isn't fair, to keep such a large secret away from her. But telling her—saying the words out loud . . . I don't think that's something I can do.

I've never been afraid to speak my mind before in my life. That's what feels worse than anything else. Silencing myself, when I've so often fought to be heard against people like Missus Wilhelmina and Anise Fowler and her hyenas. They aren't telling me to shut up now. I'm telling myself. I'm a traitor to my own voice.

I lay on my bed, on my back, with my arms spread like I'm on the cross, staring at the cracks in my ceiling. Those cracks have been made from the earthquakes this island has. There are hundreds of earthquakes every day—that's what my mom told me—but we can't feel them all, because they're so small. But those earthquakes send cracks up through the dirt and into the concrete. I watch those cracks now, watch them good, like I'm daring them to crumble this house on top of me and bury me alive.

The cracks don't dare to do any such thing. I roll onto my stomach and pick up the purple journal that's been resting at my bedside since the night I threw it like I meant to throw it out of this world and into another. Pick it up and stare at the blank paper, and as I stare, words start falling across the paper.

It's not a letter to my ma at all. It's a letter to Kalinda. And it's telling her the things I'm too afraid to say out loud. It says:

I love you, Kalinda, and I wish that we could one day be married and live together for the rest of our lives. I would love to wake up and see you in the morning, and lie down for bed at night and have you be the last thing I see before I close my eyes. You have brought me joy, and I thank you for that, and I wish that I could continue to feel this joy every day for the rest of my life. I know that we could not live as husband and wife, but that wouldn't matter, because I would be with you, and you would be with me too. It's painful that I cannot have this. I wish I could have both this and my mother, and I wish I did not have to choose, but I do have to choose, and I do have to choose my mother, because she is my mother. But if I didn't have to choose, I would hope that we could live like this, two people in love with each other, and that you could feel the same way about me too. The possibility that you could feel the same way gives me an unending hope. Leaving this island will be the second most painful day of my entire life, the first most painful day being when I woke up to find that my *mother had gone. I don't want to say good-bye to you. I've never dreaded anything more. I love you a thousand times, and a thousand times more.*

That is what the letter says, and what a thing to say too—but I know they're words that can never leave my mouth. But this letter...

I take the journal and wrap it carefully in the best wrapping paper I can find, in the bedroom with the Christmas decorations and my mother's collection of cards. The white wrapping paper has a golden trim, and my mom would use this for Easter presents. I fold the corners of the paper around the journal just the way my mother taught me, and I hide the gift in a pocket in my bag.

Early the next morning, I end up being the first one in my classroom, breeze making goose bumps pop up all over my skin. I take out the journal and slip it right into the hollow of Kalinda's desk, next to her collection of erasers and used staples. Then I sit at my desk and wait.

I might as well be waiting for the death squad, I'm so scared. My hands won't stop shaking, so I hide them in my lap. I almost go to Kalinda's desk to take the present back three times. But then Marie Antoinette and another of Anise Fowler's friends come into the room, and I know that if they see me taking the present, they'll only accuse me of stealing something that belongs to Kalinda, and there would be a big drama I could do nothing about, and they would give the gift back to Kalinda anyway, and nothing would have changed, so I might as well leave it exactly where it is.

Kalinda walks into the room, head as high as ever, taking her time smiling and greeting everyone in the room. She leaves me for last, but I know it's only because she has the most to say to me. She takes someone else's seat beside me and takes my hand and tells me that I would never believe what has happened.

"My aunt Hortensia marched outside in the dead of night to scream at the accordion player, and she tripped over me as I was sleeping out on the front steps, and so now both my father and my father's sister are absolutely livid. What a turn of events. I never would have expected this to happen."

Throughout the whole story I'm nothing but selfish, because I want her to go to her desk and find my gift to her. It's like I've lost my voice, and her opening that journal is the only way I'll ever have it back. I don't know what she'll say once she finds it. She might laugh at me. She might tell me I'm being silly. She might decide to never speak to me again. I remember the disgust she had for the two white women holding each other's hands, and I think to myself that I'm a fool to ever hope Kalinda could have a different reaction for me. Kalinda squeezes my hand and gives me my smile and only leaves my side when Missus Wilhelmina marches into the classroom.

I'd already learned by now that I could try to come up with every possible outcome, positive or negative, and try to account for every scenario that's currently playing in the infinite number of universes, and no matter what fate would find an outcome that I hadn't been expecting at all. Kalinda doesn't notice the present for the entirety of the class period with Missus Wilhelmina. She stands up for recess without the smallest glance. She looks over her shoulder at me impatiently, and so I hurry to follow her outside into the hot sun. We sit in the shade of the barren mango tree, not speaking at all about the ghosts or demons or spirit world that may or may not exist, even though I know this must be in the back of her mind as much as it is mine. Perhaps we're only giving each other a break—a chance to pretend my journey into the spirit world will not happen—and we'll be able to live happily ever after.

And when we come back in from recess a few minutes early just so we can get out of the sun, in Anise Fowler's hand is the journal, out of its wrapping paper, open in the palm of her hand like a Bible, the hyenas crowded around her while she reads her scripture. She reads something, whispering with a grin spread across her face, and the hyenas split into an uproarious screaming fit of laughter. Then they quiet again and listen to Anise's whisper, and the laughter breaks out once more.

I stand still, my heart pounding to the beat of a death march. Boom. Boom. Boom. Kalinda looks at me, putting her hand on the side of my arm, shaking it and asking me something, but I don't know what, because all I can hear is that boom against my chest. Heat fills my eyes, but before it spills over and runs all down my face, I wipe them against the side of my arm and turn to her quick. "Let's go back outside," I tell her.

"But the bell is about to ring. Missus Wilhelmina—"

"Let's find my mom now."

"Now?"

"Right now."

"It's not the eclipse."

"There has to be another way."

Kalinda looks frozen, like she doesn't know what to say. "Are you all right, Caroline?"

At the sound of my name, the hyenas transform into wolves, spinning in their seats. Anise gently closes the journal, done with reading her scripture for the day.

"Caroline Murphy," she says.

Kalinda looks to me. "What's going on?" she whispers.

"Caroline Murphy," Anise says again.

"You should take a step away from her," one of the hyenas says. It's clear that she's speaking not to me but to Kalinda.

Kalinda looks to me and to the journal Anise is holding. She's already putting two and two together.

"You know what she thinks about you?" Anise says.

The way she says it has Kalinda looking at me, hurt, like maybe I betrayed her in that journal. Like maybe I wrote horrible things about her, secrets or lies, because I've hated her all this time. I would've preferred that to what's really in there in Anise's hands right now. Anise's grin is as sharp as a knife. "Or maybe you think the same way about her?"

I'm expecting the hyenas to laugh, but this is a very serious accusation. They look at Kalinda expectantly, waiting for her to answer.

"I don't know what's in the journal," she finally says. It's the first time I've ever heard her voice quiver in my life.

"Then come and take a look," Anise says with a smile. I try to pull on Kalinda's arm, to shake my head, plead with her by squeezing her hand, but I stop when I see the way the hyenas look at me, and when I see the way Kalinda looks at me too. Reprovingly. She might as well tell me in her adult voice to stop it, stop it now, stop acting like a child. She steps away from me and to the circle of hyenas, and she's enveloped by them as Anise walks to her, holding the journal like it's a sacrifice in her hands.

There's silence, and salt stinging my eyes, though I won't let the salt fall, and I think my heart must've stopped because I don't hear it anymore now.

'Cause you'll never love again.

Kalinda looks up from the journal, and I know she's read everything on that page. She shuts the journal herself and steps out of the circle without looking at me and walks out of the room. There's a moment of silence. And then the hyenas jump to circle me instead, all of them attacking at once, saying I'm going to hell and they should light me on fire now to get a head start, and Anise starts a game where they shove me like a ball, bouncing from girl to girl, until I trip and fall and bust my knee on the floor. Then Anise drags me up by my hair and the game starts all over again. And I let them play it, because I'm not sure anything else at all matters anymore.

CHAPTER
7

Kalinda won't look at me for the whole of the day, and when Missus Wilhelmina tells us to go home, she leaps out of her seat and walks so fast she might as well have run out the classroom door. Anise stays behind, waiting for me in the courtyard. She and the hyenas march behind me all the way to waterfront, telling me to get ready to burn in hell, and that I'm disgusting, and that I shouldn't even be alive. I'm starting to think that they might be right. When the woman in black wavers in the corner of my eye, I don't even look her way.

The next morning, I don't get out of bed. Mister Lochana will wonder why I didn't come to him, and my father will get a phone call from Miss Joe tonight, hearing that this was my third strike and that I unfortunately have been expelled, but I don't care. I sleep like the little white girl slept in that fairy tale for what feels like a hundred years.

When I wake up, the sun has already set and is beginning to rise again. I leave my house and walk out into the yellow sun, walk and walk and walk down the road. Like she's waiting for me, Bernadette is sitting right there in a guava tree. She looks like she's a little girl ghost. She swings her legs back and forth, and while they swing I could swear both her hands are on backward, as are her feet.

"Why you can't just stay away from here?" I ask. She just keeps swinging her legs. I pick up the biggest stone I can find and throw it. It misses her head by a good foot. I wish I could say I meant to miss, but I don't think I did.

"I came here to meet my father, but now I have to go home again."

"Why would I care about something like that?" I ask.

"Because your father is my father." And when I don't say anything, she adds, "We're sisters."

"What?"

"You're my big sister," she says. "I'm your little sister. That's what my mom tells me."

"Your mom's a liar."

She jumps down from the tree and opens her mouth and lets out such a scream that I'm sure the gates of hell are ripping open. I slap my hands over my ears, and she keeps screaming and screaming.

"Shut up!" I yell, but she pays me no mind. She takes a big breath and starts her screaming all over again, tracks of tears and snot running all down her face. Anyone would swear I'd tried to kill her mother dead instead of called her a liar. I can't take it anymore, so I turn on my heel and race up the white road to my house.

My dad comes back just when the frogs start to make their noise. He steps inside the house and stumbles a bit when he catches me sitting alone in the dark. He doesn't say anything as he walks inside and turns on the light and drops his keys on the countertop with a clatter. He comes back inside and sniffs as he kicks off his shoes and leans back in his chair and unfolds a three-day-old newspaper.

"Your principal called me at work," he says. "She wanted to know why you haven't been at school. I told her you were sick."

I know I should thank him. He's probably expecting

me to thank him, apologize, and explain what happened. Or maybe he's expecting his little rebellious Caroline tonight. Maybe he thinks I'll start to yell and scream and cuss him out. Instead, I say something he isn't expecting at all.

"That little girl down the road said I'm her sister."

He looks up at me. Sniffs again and turns the page of his newspaper. "That's true."

I think about that story Kalinda told me, with the spot of rage anyone felt if they ever walked through it in the library in Barbados, and I wonder for a second if maybe that ghost got to me now from all the way across the sea—but no, that rage is coming from me, so violently that maybe when I'm dead this very spot will become the same, and anytime anyone walks through here, they'll wish they could see their father dead.

Mine starts to cry now. I never really expected to see such a thing in my life, but that's what he's doing: He's sitting there and crying and pretending he's not, as he keeps holding up the newspaper. His hands are shaking and his eyes are filling and I tell myself I'm so angry that I don't care, he could cry himself to death and I wouldn't care one bit, but my heart starts to ache too, and then my eyes start to sting.

"Is that why she left? Is that why my ma left us?"

He can't even speak or nod or shake his head, so I ask again where my ma is, and he opens his mouth and says it so quiet I almost don't hear the words: "She's here."

*

It should be a relief, and for a minute it is—my mother wasn't taken by the woman in black. She isn't trapped in the spirit world, and I won't have to travel through the eclipse to become stuck there for the rest of my life too. But then the questions start to come. How long has she been back? If she's back, why hasn't she come to me? Why hasn't she come back home to see me? Even if she never wants to see my father ever again, I have done nothing wrong to her. If she's back in the Virgin Islands, then she should have come to see me and take me away with her so we can start a new and happy life together.

My father only told me that she's here, in the Virgin

Islands, on Saint Thomas—not that she's alive. I can only think of one explanation for why my mother hasn't come back for me, and that explanation requires her to be six feet under the ground.

*

My father doesn't have to force me to go to school the next morning. I need to get out of the house so that's what I do. Anise and Marie Antoinette and their friends are waiting for me. Anise starts to yell I shouldn't go to this school because it's a Catholic school, and sinners shouldn't attend Catholic schools, and she says too that I shouldn't be allowed into the church, because that's no place for sinners either, but today there's too much on my mind for me to even listen. Maybe it's my blank stare— that I'm looking past them, staring at the little dead girl that looks like my sister standing in the middle of the courtyard. I don't respond. I don't even look their way. Anise just becomes quiet on her own, and they stare at me silently like I'm a dead girl too, laying in an open casket as they all march past at my viewing.

As soon as Kalinda walks into our classroom, I'm on

my feet and by her side and ignoring all the stares that follow. I can only see her face.

She's not looking at me, but she doesn't try to push past me as if I don't exist, the way she acted two days ago—the way I thought she would this morning too. Relief threads its way through me. Kalinda mumbles a good morning.

"Good morning," I say to her. I take in a sharp breath. "My mother is on island."

Her eyes snap to me. "What? How do you know?"

"I have a sister who told me, and my father finally admitted it, and now that she's on island—I have to find her."

She nods, then looks past me, noticing the faces that are turned in our direction. She swallows and looks away again. "I'll speak to you after school." Then she goes to her seat and does not turn to whisper anything to me for the entirety of the school day.

*

Kalinda is waiting for me after school, like she promised. We walk through town, and at first I think she's bringing me to her house, but we keep walking right by. I shouldn't be surprised. She will probably never invite me to her house ever again.

"I'll help you find your mother, because I know that's the right thing to do," she tells me, "but I don't know if I can be your friend."

The pain that spreads through me is paralyzing. I stop walking.

"Is it because of that letter?" I say. I try to think of something—anything—to say about that letter. "It was just a joke. But then Anise found it, and she—"

"I know that's not true," she says.

I quiet myself.

"It's wrong for one girl to feel that way about another," she says gravely. "You know that, don't you, Caroline?"

I could cry, my spirit hurts so bad. "That's what I've been told, but I don't believe every single little thing anyone tells me."

"You're a Christian, aren't you? Don't you believe in God?"

"White people once used the Bible to say that we should be slaves."

"What does that have anything to do with this?"

"Everything," I tell her. "It means we should think for ourselves. Decide if something is wrong just because someone says it's so, or decide it's right because that's how we feel."

She looks me over, up and down. "I wish I could think the same way." And she keeps walking, and I'm not at all sure what she meant by this, but it leaves my heart stuttering.

"And so your mother is back on island."

"Yes" is all I tell her.

"Well? You must know more. What's your plan now? I can't help you if all you know is that she's on this island."

And it looks to me like Kalinda doesn't have any patience to help me find a plan, either. If I tell her that I don't have one, she might just walk away from me right here, right now, and never speak to me again. It isn't lost on me that somehow all my wishes were granted: My mother is on island, and Kalinda is here too. There is still a hope, a chance, that Kalinda might someday return my feelings, and I'll have the unending joy of being able to love her, and being able to have my mother.

If she's still alive. If she isn't now trapped in a graveyard.

I rummage through my mind and come up with an answer quick. "I need evidence that she's still alive, and if she's still alive, then I need to know where she is. My dad is hiding that from me. And now, Miss Joe is too."

"What will you do?"

I think of my dad's room. Even though he caught me, I managed to get through a lot of his closet, his drawers—enough to see that he didn't really keep papers there, no letters or documents that would prove my mom was still alive, or that she was still in contact with him.

I decide it right then and there. "I want to spy on Miss Joe," I tell her. "She's hiding something from me. I want to know what it is."

Kalinda is good at hiding her expressions and emotions, as adults often are. If she's surprised or upset hearing this, she doesn't show it. She only nods.

"Then I'll do what I can to help," she says.

CHAPTER

Breaking into Miss Joe's office isn't as easy as I thought it would be, seeing that she always keeps her door wide open for anyone to come in, even when she isn't there. The problem is that she *is* always there, or it seems like it that morning as she sits and reads her newspaper and eats her hot cereal. Kalinda and I have already missed one full class with Missus Wilhelmina, and when she asks where we are, the other children will say they never saw the two of us at all this morning, since we have been hiding in the empty classroom that's directly beside Miss Joe's office, staring through tiny holes in the wall, and when Missus Wilhelmina hears that, she'll immediately call our homes, only to hear that we've left as we were supposed to (or hear it from Kalinda's anyway, since no one will be at my home to answer the phone), and so the search will be on. We don't have very much time, and I'm nervous that if I'm caught, this really will be my third strike, and Miss Joe will send me home just as she promised, away from the first friend I've ever made and quite possibly the love of my life, and away from the one chance I have to learn the truth about my mother.

Finally, Missus Wilhelmina comes right into the office, just as I thought she would, and my heart drops—but instead of my name coming from her mouth, she throws up her hands and complains that one of the overhead fans has broken, and she and her class of students are destined to die of heatstroke if they're forced to sit in that classroom any longer, so Miss Joe heaves a sigh and stands from her desk to follow Missus Wilhelmina away. I look at Kalinda and she nods. This is our only chance.

We leave the empty office and run into Miss Joe's room. The mountains of teetering books, the scraps of paper that seem to be flying in every which way, the mess itself—I remember what Miss Joe's office is like, but I never until this moment understood how incredibly packed it is with papers, and how impossible it'll be to find anything at all. Maybe this is why Miss Joe has no qualms about leaving her door unlocked. She knows thieves won't be able to find anything anyway.

"I'll begin over here," I tell Kalinda, who nods and goes to the opposite end of the tiny office, and I begin looking through books and papers, but of course nothing about my mother is there. Miss Joe will be back any moment. Maybe this isn't worth the risk. I stand straight and look at her desk. I go to it, and standing atop is a row of many photo frames and many smiling faces of Miss Joe throughout the years: one black-and-white picture of a girl-child version of Miss Joe standing in a somber crowd of other young girls; one brightly colored photo of an older Miss Joe holding a toddler on her hip on the sand of a beach; another of her standing tall and proud in her graduation uniform; and one yellowed photo of two young women, only slightly older than me, and one of them is undoubtedly Miss Joe, and the other is just as clearly my mother.

I hold the photo. Kalinda comes to stand beside me. "Who are they?" she asks. She's sweating, either from the heat or the exertion of rushing through books and files.

I hold up the photo and put my finger on the glass, leaving my fingerprint in a smudge. "That's my mom."

Kalinda takes the photo with a smile. "She's beautiful." She looks at me again. "You look like her."

My heart blooms like a flower in my chest. "I don't."

"You do. You have her nose and her eyes and her brows." She hands me back the photo in its frame.

I didn't realize Kalinda had studied my face so closely. I'm suddenly shy and can't look at her properly.

"Why does Miss Joe have a photo of your mother?" she asks.

"They were best friends," I tell her, and almost add, *and they were in love.* "I'll keep this," I say.

"You'll steal it? Won't Miss Joe notice?"

She probably will, but I don't have a photo of my mom. She never took any for my dad and me, and though this isn't the face I know, it's still her face. "She might, but I don't care. I want to keep it."

Voices come down the hall, one of a woman complaining about something we can't hear, and I know immediately it's Missus Wilhelmina and Miss Joe returning.

I take Kalinda's hand and we rush out the room quick as lightning, but they're already so close that they see us, and Missus Wilhelmina yells and screams and tries to run after us, but we run so fast back to her classroom that she isn't able to follow or see where we've gone. By the time she returns, we're already sitting in the classroom, sweating with the rest of the class, though no one else will have known it was from running. The second we exploded into the room, Kalinda begged them all to lie for us and say that we have always been there, and though no one likes me, they all like Kalinda, and so the entire class agreed.

Missus Wilhelmina walks back in and immediately comes to a stop beside my desk. "Where were you, Miss Murphy?"

"I was always here."

The class hesitates, and then Anise agrees loudly. "She was always here stinking up the room."

They all laugh.

Missus Wilhelmina looks confused. She crosses her arms. "I would've remembered you being here. I even thought to myself that you were not."

I force on the most confused face I can muster. "I was always here, Missus Wilhelmina."

Everyone else nods their agreement. Missus Wilhelmina frowns at me until she goes to the front of the classroom.

"Two students were seen running from Miss Joe's office."

Everyone gasps and eyes swing to Kalinda and me, but no one says anything.

"Nothing was taken, but if these students are ever found, believe me and God, they will not be coming back to this school. Do you hear me?"

We all murmur, "Yes, Missus Wilhelmina."

She looks pleased and so begins her lesson once again. Neither Kalinda nor I dare to look at each other for the rest of the period.

*

I'm home, laying on my back on my bed, holding the photo in its frame high above me. The frame is silver and rusted, with the paint scraped away from its edges. The color of the photo is brown and white, and it's yellowed with old age. My mother and Miss Joe are posing together, their flowery skirts flaring out around their knees, and I see that Miss Joe's are swollen, and that my mom's knees look like round rocks sticking out from her skin, just like my own. They stand side by side, their hands folded together in front of their stomachs as proper young ladies should place them, but their smiles aren't genteel and poised. They look like they're about to burst out laughing and they're trying their best not to. Seeing them like this, I don't know whether I want to laugh or cry myself.

I want to know what the photo feels like—want to touch it, because then maybe that'd mean I'm touching something my mother has touched, and want to smell it, because maybe it somehow still smells like my mother too, like the scent of her perfume. I pull and tug the back of the frame until it creaks open, and then slide the photo out gently so it won't tear. The paper is surprisingly rough, and the photo smells like mothballs—not like my mother at all.

I flip it over, and on the back are yellow stains and cursive writing in pencil that has almost faded away.

I hold it close to my eyes to see more clearly. It says: *Doreen Hendricks residence, 5545 Mariendahl, 19th of September, 1974.*

I run my finger over the writing. 5545 Mariendahl? I flip the photo over again, and see that they're standing in front of a house that looks to have a short roof and wide windows, and though I've never seen this house before, I'm willing to bet anything that its address is 5545 Mariendahl. And I don't know for sure if this is where I can find my mother—but I also know it's the only clue I have.

*

The next morning, I walk out before the sun is in the sky, when it's still hidden behind the green hills, and the clouds are pink and the birds have just started to sing their songs, and I walk to the guava tree to find Bernadette. She isn't there, swinging her legs or grinning with her too-big teeth, so I keep walking the road until it takes me up the hill and back down again. The little house where she was living is empty now, its windows so black it's like no one ever lived there at all.

The photo is still in my hand. What was I going to do? Ask Bei edette if she knew of this house? Go there myself, if s d me yes, that's where   mother could be found? If   up to this house too   and knocked on the door so it would swing open and reveal my mother standing there, looking down at me like a stranger, I'm not sure I would have anymore a reason to stay alive. If my mother opens the door, and she can't tell me why she hasn't come back for me in all this time, I think I really might as well just let myself die. Nobody but my mother has ever loved me, and if she doesn't love me anymore, I have not a soul on this Earth that cares anything about me. No one cares about someone like me, and no one cares that I'm angry about that either. Might as well be the crazy man screaming at everyone around him, or might as well not exist at all. And so I think maybe I really don't belong to this world. Now, that's a lonely thought.

*

When I come to school, I sit alone in the classroom with my head bent low. The photo is still in the pocket of my skirt. No one has anything to say to me today. Anise Fowler and her friends leave me alone. I don't even feel their stares. This is a strange and unprecedented thing, but I wonder if it's because of the way I've stared blankly past them, and because of the way Kalinda asked them to help me just yesterday. We're not friends, and never will be, but maybe now we're not quite hated enemies, either.

Someone stops beside my desk, and I look up to see Kalinda. She doesn't look like she knows for sure what she wants to say to me.

"Good morning," she says.

I tell her good morning too.

She stands there, the expression on her face pained. She looks like she doesn't know if she should stay or run away. Finally she opens her mouth. "Have you found anything?" she asks. "Anything about your mother?"

I don't want to tell her the truth. If I do, then we'll have to go to 5545 Mariendahl Road together, and I'll have to see my mother opening the door and looking at me without any love in her eyes, and then once we've found her, Kalinda won't have any reason to speak to me anymore. I grip my hands and shake my head.

She still stands beside me. She rocks back and forth on her heels and her toes. "I tried to imagine myself not speaking to you at all today," she says. "I'd come here planning to ignore you."

This hurts my heart more than I can bear, so I look away, expecting that she'll take her leave. But she stays where she is—even continues to speak.

"But the second I arrived and saw you, I knew that I couldn't ignore you, no matter how much I tried." She pauses for a long while before she asks, "Would you like to take a walk with me after school?"

I'm surprised. I look to Anise, who has her back turned to us. I'm not sure I trust this. Would it be possible that Anise convinced Kalinda to play a cruel game on me? That she's only pretending to be my friend again? "Why?"

"Because we need to talk," she says. "I have some things to say to you."

I'm afraid. I don't want to know what she wants to say, or whether she even speaks the truth or not. But I nod my head anyway, unable to really look at her. I stare at the air over her shoulder instead. She turns on her heel and returns to her seat, and doesn't say a single word to me for the rest of the day—not until I find her waiting for me on the church's front steps.

"I thought we could walk to the beach," she tells me as she starts the walk. "I haven't been swimming in a very long time."

I wring my hands together. "I don't want to swim," I tell her.

"Why not?"

"I'm afraid of the ocean."

"Is that so?"

"Yes," I say, and I remind her of the day I fell off Mister Lochana's speedboat and nearly drowned before I'd even had a chance to fully learn how to walk.

"Well," she says, "I won't let you drown."

She keeps walking, like that should be enough. Who knows? Maybe it is. In fact, I decide that, yes, I'm safe when I'm with Kalinda, and if it turns out that this really is nothing more than a cruel game, then I'll have nothing else in this world at all, because right now, I think she is the only other person I can trust besides myself.

We walk and walk and walk, all down through town and past the graveyard and over the long strips of paved road where mirages shimmer in the sun. The sky has gray clouds blowing in from the west, and with them comes the smell of rain and a heaviness in the air, but Kalinda doesn't seem to care. She just keeps on walking. She doesn't speak to me. She only walks with such a focused look on her face that I think she'll just leave me behind if I don't keep up.

When we get to the beach, sand spilling onto the road, she doesn't waste any time. She takes off her shoes and socks and places them neatly in the shade of a palm tree and runs straight for the water. I do the same, hot sand burning my feet, and follow her. She leaps into the waves and comes back up again, her locks flying with salt water everywhere. I stop where the water crashes onto the sand, foaming up around my toes, trying to suck me back out again.

She stands in the water. Stands like she's a queen of the spirit world. Kalinda doesn't belong here. I know that for sure.

"Come," she says. "I won't let anything bad happen to you."

I wade into the waves after her, the cold winter water lapping up against my thighs and my sides, making my school uniform stick to my skin. Kalinda takes my hand.

"I'm sorry for the way I treated you," she says.

"It's okay," I say automatically, even if it isn't true.

"I've thought long and hard about our friendship, Caroline, and I realized that I miss you too much to lose you. I still want to be your friend, if you'll let me—even if what you feel is a sin."

There's pain mixed with joy that strings around my heart, caging it in so it can only beat a low thump—pain that she does not love me as I love her, pain that she thinks my love for her is a sin ... but joy that she considers me her friend once again. It begins to rain, lashing water against our skin and making the sea splash into our hair, and even then we just stay in the water together. "I'd love to be your friend, Kalinda."

When we leave the beach, she takes my hand and walks me to waterfront, and stands there and watches me leave on Mister Lochana's speedboat. I think about how

I hope she can do that every afternoon—walk me to waterfront and say good-bye and watch me as if she'll stand there until I've returned in the morning again. And then when we've both gotten old enough, maybe she can get onto Mister Lochana's boat with me, and we can go to my home together, and she can live there with me until I've returned in the morning again.

*

The next morning, when I walk into the classroom, I expect to see her sitting in her seat, eagerly waiting for me in the same way that I'm eagerly waiting to see her, but she isn't there.

You ain't got no one to hold you.

And she doesn't come, not even when the school bell rings. She's never been late before, and others have noticed too. Heads turn to her empty seat. Missus Wilhelmina walks into the classroom and stands in the center, right in front of the blackboard, and announces that Kalinda won't be a student here anymore.

You ain't got no one to care.

That her family is taking her back to Barbados now.

And she promptly begins her lesson for the day.

Kalinda is gone. My mother is gone. I have no friends. I am all alone again, as it seems I always have been, and always will be, except for the woman in black, who I know will never leave.

CHAPTER

I don't even wait for the school day to end. I slip out of my seat and find myself in front of Kalinda's house, shouting her name. "Kalinda! Kalinda!" There's a rush of wind that carries my voice away, so I scream louder. "Kalinda Francis!"

Finally the door opens, and Kalinda stands on her porch above me like she wants to know who in the world could possibly be shouting like the devil. When she sees it's me, she doesn't look completely surprised. She's only a little surprised. She leaves her porch and walks down the stairs where she says she finds herself sleeping at night, and opens the gate and stops right in front of me.

"I wasn't planning on saying good-bye like this," she tells me.

"You mean you weren't planning on saying good-bye at all!"

"We had our good-bye yesterday."

"Yesterday can't count if only one person knows they're saying good-bye."

She seems to think about this for a moment. A hard breeze makes her locks swing through the air. "Maybe so," she finally says, "but I thought it might be less painful this way. I hate saying good-byes, you know."

For a moment, I can't even look at her. I'm so furious that my hands are shaking. She said so many things to me, and she knew that she was leaving, so all those things were nothing but lies. I turn to the side so I can stare at her house instead. "When are you leaving?"

"In two days."

"Then we have two days to find my mother."

She gives me a funny look. "I can't help you do that," she says.

"You made me a promise."

"Things have changed. I have to go to Barbados."

"I expect you to keep that promise."

"There's a storm coming, you know," she says.

154

I did not know, but I don't care. I was born of a storm. Storms don't scare me.

"We'll both be in trouble," she says.

I do know this, but I don't care about that, either. I'm always in trouble.

Kalinda has run out of reasons to stay. I've finally turned back to her, and she's looking at me now too.

"Please," I say, so quiet I don't think she's even heard me.

But then she nods. "Okay. But if we're going to go, we have to go now."

That works just fine for me.

*

We don't bring any clothes or any food. Kalinda doesn't go back upstairs to her house, because if she does, then there's a chance she won't be able to leave again. So the two of us start walking right there and then.

I take out the photo, which now has a permanent home in my pocket, and as we walk I show it to Kalinda so she can also see its back.

"Fifty-five forty-five Mariendahl, nineteenth of

September, nineteen seventy-four," she reads. She flips it over and stares at the photo. "Is this where you'll find your mother?"

"I think so," I tell her.

"I think so too," she says.

*

We will go to 5545 Mariendahl, but the sun is getting lower in the sky, and the mosquitoes are coming out to find us, and Kalinda says that nighttime is when the spirits will come out to find us too. Night is when the angriest ones come around, ready to get their revenge on anyone who is still alive. She says we need to find a place to hide, and then we will go to 5545 Mariendahl Road in the countryside first thing in the morning.

She takes us down to Havensight Dock, the dock where cruise ships let tourists on and off. Cruise ships pass by Water Island every morning. Their horns are my alarm clocks. At night, their lights glow like a thousand little suns. They are moving cities, the glass and steel compacted onto a single boat. Surrounding Havensight Dock are shops filled with tourist souvenirs: T-shirts reading I CAME, I SAW, I TOOK PICTURES! ST. THOMAS, USVI and photos of naked women on beaches and postcards with men with long locks, even longer than Kalinda's, and chickens. I think that I once saw Mister Lochana on one of those postcards, and sometimes Oprah the donkey is featured too.

We walk through the stores, ignoring the angry eye the shopkeepers give us. They don't like too many locals in their stores when they are trying to sell to tourists, and they hate children still in their school uniforms who aren't going to buy anything at all. They watch us good until we leave.

Farther beyond the tourist shops are newly built condos that no one but celebrities from the States are rich enough to use. I heard that Oprah—the real Oprah—once stayed in one of those condos. From what my pa said, though, she's the only one that's ever stayed there. No one wants to stay in those condos.

Right across the street are the housing projects, repainted to match the dull beige of the condos, with beautiful murals that were added to every single wall when the condos were built so when tourists and celebrities passed by the housing projects, they wouldn't know what they were seeing.

"How is it that those condos are empty," Kalinda says, "and across the street they've got eight people in a room?"

"I think I have an idea," I say.

"Let's hear it, then."

"No one's living in there, right? We should stay in there for the night."

"I don't know if we should mess with those condos."

"Are you afraid?" I tease.

"Yes," she says. "If we mess with those condos"—and she pauses here for effect—"they'll beat us till we bleed."

"They'll do more than beat us if they catch us. They'll throw us into jail."

"They can't put us in jail," Kalinda says. "We're too young."

I hate being corrected. "You can go right on ahead and stay outside for the night, then, if you're too scared."

"Not scared," Kalinda says. "Just smart."

"It's just for a night," I say. "No one would even know."

She shakes her head. "You're out of your mind."

I smile. "You don't have to do a single thing if you don't want to," I say. "But me—I'll be living like a queen tonight."

I turn away from her, pretending that I don't care if she follows me or not. I don't turn around when I hear her coming. We walk down the sidewalk, across the street from the housing projects. Keeping us out of the condos is the black iron fence with sharp spikes at the top. We pass by a security box right by the locked gate. The box is as big as a man, and the officer inside is being baked alive in his uniform. He shines with sweat as he fans himself with the pages of a book. He watches a cricket game on a little TV. We walk by him so slowly that he gets suspicious. He pokes his head out the open window. He isn't a happy man, sitting in a small sweltering box, guarding an empty condominium.

Kalinda and I speed up our walk. I look over my shoulder to see the security guard watching us until we pass the black gate altogether. The second we pass the sidewalk, he goes back to fanning himself and watching his handheld TV.

"In here, quick," I say as the second the security guard looks away.

I take Kalinda around the corner and alongside the gate that leads into the unpaved field and trees and pipes that spill out to the ocean and isn't covered with concrete. "He can't see us here, right?"

Kalinda scours the bottom of the iron fence. Finally she points out a hole that's been dug out by an iguana. We get through easily with only a few scratches on our arms, and when we're on the other side of the gate, we run until we're sweating and we can't breathe without bending over and putting our hands on our knees. I'm gasping for breath when I stand to see. There is an untouched stone path that takes us through the budding gardens that are well-kept for the people who don't live there. Red hibiscus that iguana like to eat are small flames, and trees with flower petals falling with every light breeze make me feel like I've stepped into another world entirely.

We bend low beneath the neatly clipped bush, listening for the footsteps of concealed security guards. At the end of the path, we take turns poking our heads out past the edge of the hedge's leaves. When we're confident that we're the only ones there, we leave the path and walk into the courtyard.

It isn't like the church's courtyard, with ancient cobblestones and bird droppings. This courtyard is a garden of grass and roses, a gazebo with benches and a sleepily rotating fan. No clouds in the sky, so the blue that is the color of the ocean reflects off of the leaves, turned honey by the yellow sun. The courtyard overlooks a dock. The dock is private for the condos. The water is clear, and we can smell its salt. Kalinda runs right through that garden and jumps into the sea. She sinks and floats to the top with a smile. I sit on the edge of the concrete dock, rough beneath my thighs, my toes scraping the edge of the water. I watch Kalinda swim and dive until I'm tired of watching. With my loafers in my hand, I walk through the garden. The path continues to the other end of the iron gate, but from where I stand, I can't see the security guard anywhere.

And in front of me are the condominiums. There are five in all, and the main one—the one I'm sure Oprah

Winfrey stayed in—stares down at us with its beige paint and white trim, gold handles for the glass French doors. Sweeping staircases lead to the upper level, which has a balcony and white wicker chairs.

I run up the stairs and go to the doors. I'm not surprised when they're locked. I can see Kalinda swimming beneath the glass waves. There are windows on either side of the door. I yank one up, and then push on the mosquito screen behind it. I push hard enough that the screen falls to the floor with a clatter.

I climb inside. The white tile is cold beneath my feet. I smell dust and dried paint. The walls are yellow, to match the sunshine, and there are couches bigger than my bed. The couches face a television, so wide it almost covers the entire wall. I grab a remote that's neatly placed on the glass coffee table and throw myself on a couch that squeaks beneath my bum. I flip through movie stations, hundreds of them. I watch until I hear a knock on the door.

I jump; I can't help it, and I don't like the way Kalinda laughs at me, her head poking through the window. I get up and open the door for her. She walks into the room and gestures at the TV. "These are all the stations my father won't buy." And she walks away, down the hall, opening each door and oohing and aahing, until she opens one door and calls the Lord's name in vain. When I follow her to see what she's staring at, I can't help but call the Lord's name too.

The bedroom is as big as my house. It has a ceiling so high I feel like I'm in church, and the one bed has see-through sheets covering it so it shimmers in the light of the window. Kalinda runs to that bed so fast that when she lands, she bounces high into the air. I follow, and we jump and bounce on the bed until I fall off with a thud that shakes the whole room. Even I have to laugh, rolling around on the floor.

When our laughing gets quiet, we stay still, staring at whatever it is we're staring at. I'm staring out at the ocean. I can see the green mirage of Saint John. Closer to Saint Thomas is Water Island. I can see it just fine from the window. If I look hard enough, I can probably see my house too, and see the window that looks into the kitchen, and see my pa sitting at the table, waiting for his two women to come home.

*

Night is coming. I can tell from the way the sky starts to turn colors like a kaleidoscope. Night is when the cruise ships begin to leave. I can see them at Havensight Dock, backing away from Saint Thomas slowly. It's peaceful, watching them, until the horns go off like sirens, so loud they hurt my teeth. The walls and floor shudder, and Kalinda and I both cover our ears. When the horns stop, we're still there with our hands covering our ears, and we laugh at each other. And I think suddenly that if I love Kalinda, maybe there's a chance Kalinda loves me too, and maybe we could share our first kiss together—maybe she could even become my wife—but I get too scared to even mention such a possibility, and instead we smile at each other in the quiet.

We get hungry, so we go downstairs to the kitchen to see if Oprah left any good food behind. The cabinets are only filled with hurricane food: cold Vienna sausage, stale crackers, and gallons of water.

"There isn't anything else?" I ask. I always get a little bad-tempered whenever I'm hungry.

"I'm afraid not," Kalinda says.

We pop open the cans and put them on the living room floor in front of the TV. The TV is the only light, because bulbs haven't been put into the lamps yet and the sun is now long gone. It starts to get cold once the sun is down and the trade wind kicks up from the Arctic over the ocean and comes right into the condo. Since Kalinda is still wet from her swim by the docks, she starts sneezing and coughing. We watch white people on the TV screen for a while, but even the movies with guns and fast cars and explosions get boring after a while.

"My auntie and dad are going to be so pissed," Kalinda says.

I don't know what my pa will do. My ma was the one to discipline me, and depending on my crime, I had a good idea of what my punishment would be. Bad grades meant no television; not eating my dinner meant no dessert. Talking back meant a slap across the mouth, but I never liked talking back to my ma that much when she was around. I liked listening to her when she told me to do something—wash the dishes, clean my room—because I liked the smile she had for me when I was done. When she left, my pa tried telling me to do the same things, but he didn't have a smile for me at the end of it, so I stopped doing what he said.

"We should go to bed," Kalinda says. "We'll have a long day tomorrow."

We turn off the television and climb into bed. Kalinda is still wet, so the dampness spreads from her and onto the sheets so, before long, I'm shivering too. Kalinda notices. She takes me into her arms, but since her skin is cold too, we do nothing but shiver together.

*

When I wake up, it's to a voice. I think Kalinda has woken up before me and turned on the TV, but when I open my eyes, I see that she's still asleep, turned over and with her arms covering her face from the light coming in through the balcony doors. I sit up to figure out where the voice came from. I freeze when I see the security guard. It's the same one who'd been sitting in his hot box. He must have been going from condo to condo to make sure that the iguanas didn't manage to get in.

He stands at the door, yelling and cussing us good. "You want to go to jail, eh?" he asks. "You want to go to jail!"

Kalinda wakes up not a heartbeat later. When she opens her eyes and sees the guard, she gets out of bed carefully, eyes on the security guard's baton, which is gripped in a meaty hand.

"You're coming with me," the guard says over and over again. He stands in front of the doorway, and the only other way out is by jumping off the balcony and into the garden below. When Kalinda and I look at each other, we only have a second. We run at the guard and push him so hard that he lands on his back. Kalinda grabs my arm and pulls me out of the room, but the guard grabs her ankle. She falls hard to the ground. I double back and jump so I land on the guard's stomach. He yells out and grabs me by my knees with his sweaty palms, but lets go when I kick him in his nose. He screams that I broke it— that I broke his nose—and Kalinda and I run, yelling at the top of our lungs, past our mess of empty Vienna sausage cans in the living room and down the stairs and out into the garden.

"We have to go to the hole," Kalinda says. I know she's right, so I start off for the black iron fence. Kalinda runs faster than me and gets to the iguana hole first. There's a yelling. The security guard, hand over his bleeding nose, stumbles down the stairs and makes his way toward us.

Both Kalinda and I dive through the hole, scratching ourselves up on the rocks and getting my shirt and skirt caked with dirt. Kalinda rushes forward and jumps onto a taxi, and she grabs my hand and pulls me up. We look back at the black iron gate and the condos. The security guard has just reached the fence.

It takes us a moment, but when the taxi reaches waterfront, the two of us start laughing. We laugh so hard that we get tears in our eyes. The other passengers just watch us all the way into the countryside.

CHAPTER

10

The wind is stronger. The sky is gray. Water begins to fall to the ground in great big plops. The woman driving the taxi stops under a swinging streetlight, and me and Kalinda jump off without paying. She calls out to us, but she doesn't cuss us like I thought she would. She tells us to get home soon.

"There's a tropical storm coming," she says. "Haven't you heard?"

Kalinda and I stand on the side of the road, and the water begins to fall harder, soaking my shirt and lashing my face. She takes my hand.

"Are you nervous?"

I nod.

"Are you scared?"

I nod again.

She takes a deep breath. "I am too."

"Why would you be scared?" She wasn't the one meeting her mom for the first time in over a year.

"I'm scared because I have something to tell you," she says. She takes my other hand. "I'm sorry for the way I hurt you, Caroline."

"You already said that you were sorry."

"It hurt me, to see that I was hurting you. And more than that: I was afraid of the truth."

I don't let myself breathe or speak. If I do, I'm afraid Kalinda will blow away on the breeze. It's only because Kalinda watches me like she wants me to speak that I make myself say, "And what is the truth?"

She looks at me like she isn't planning on saying it, because I should know what the truth is, and maybe I should, and maybe I do—but then she decides to say it out loud anyway. "I feel the same way about you too." She's still holding my hand, and I don't know what to say, but I'm also afraid that she's going to let go, so I grip her fingers in mine even tighter. She keeps speaking. "I was afraid to, because I've been told it's wrong, but you're right—I don't want to think that way, just because some-one said it's so. I know the truth. I love you."

She continues to talk—tells me how much the letter really meant to her, that she'd taken the journal home to read it over and over, and how she would like nothing more than to marry me too, one day when we're old enough. I'm still not sure if I can completely believe her, but I see the way her eyes watch me with all the grave seriousness of the entire world, and I know she means every word. I could almost cry.

Kalinda tells me that we have to keep moving, before it starts to rain, so we climb the steep hills and jump over gates and barricades and walk through the yards of aban-doned houses, whitewashed and glowing under the blind-ing sun, still shining through the clouds. My leg gets caught on a wire as I climb over a fence, cutting me sharp. Kalinda doesn't notice, and I decide not to tell her. We walk down the street, my loafers sinking into the moist dirt. Guinea grass and brush slices my shins. Cars pass by. Kalinda and I walk silently side by side.

We're in the countryside, with the hillsides that go up and back down like roller-coaster rides, and from where we can see all the islands spread out before us like we own the entire world. Missus Wilhelmina would say that it's blasphemy to think something like that, when clearly the world belongs to the Lord Jesus Christ. We can see black clouds moving in fast from the east, so we speed up our walk.

I have trouble remembering what day it is. It's been one full night since my father has seen me. I know he has to be worried, and I do feel very bad, but I need to go to 5545 Mariendahl Road, or I'm afraid I'll never want to try to find my mom again. I'll just let myself sink back into the life I had before, and I'll decide that I don't need to find my mother anymore, because I'll simply be too afraid to try, so I need to do it now, before I decide to never attempt to find her again.

We walk into the back roads and into a neighborhood hidden by brush, where a dog is tied up to a tree with a chain and some men sit on the corner playing dominoes, slapping the pieces on the board and cussing at each other as they laugh, and a broken-down car sits rusting under the sun. I look at the house numbers until I reach the one that might have my mother inside. The house has a white wall and a gate and an empty driveway. I stand there, looking at the house, and the fears come back again. The fears that she'll take one look at me and ask why I'm here. That she'll tell me she stopped loving me even before the day she left. I stand there and look at the door. It looks to me to be the most evil door in the world. It seems like any other front door, but there must be an evil spirit hiding inside of it, and once I open the door, that spirit will send me through the threshold and right into the pits of hell. I'm not at all sure what to do with a door like that.

We stand beside each other. I can hear Kalinda breathing—taking long breaths, like she's trying to calm herself. She almost looks as nervous as I am.

I unlatch the gate and walk down the path and knock on the door. I hear footsteps, and the door opens and there's a screen in between me and a woman with her braided hair tied in a bun. "Yes?" she says.

"Good afternoon," I say. "I'm looking for a Missus Doreen Murphy."

She gives me a look. "Doreen? The only Doreen I know is a Hendricks."

My heart hammers. It's true—she's here, she has to be. "Yes, that's the same one."

She shakes her head. "That's my cousin. We grew up in this house together when we were children, even though we lost touch some years ago. May I ask who you are?"

Cousin—if she's related to my mother, then this woman who I've never laid eyes on before is related to me too. "I—" I begin, but I don't know what to say. How do I explain that she's my mother, and that I'm her daughter?

"We have a gift for her, from her old friend Miss Joseph," Kalinda says, stepping forward.

"Loretta Joseph?" The woman raises her eyebrows. "Now, that's a woman I haven't heard from in years. Well, you're close enough—Doreen didn't move far. Just walk over the hill there, you see? And to the right of the mahogany tree splitting the middle of the road is a white house standing on its own, and a garden of yellow flowers. It's hard to miss it. You'll see."

We thank her and turn to leave, but not before the woman tells us to make sure we hurry. "The storm's supposed to be here before the sun sets. Best get home as quick as you can."

*

We walk up the hill, granite road turning to dust and mud and weeds, and turn down the path to the right of the mahogany tree. Standing tall before the brush is a white house with a garden of yellow flowers, and standing on the porch is a little girl. She's small, maybe five or six years old.

"Good afternoon," I say, and when she just looks up at me, I keep going. "My name is Caroline Murphy. I'm looking for someone. I'm looking for a Doreen Murphy. Doreen Hendricks. Do you know if she's here?"

The girl shakes her head. I think she might be shy. This makes me feel shy too. I suddenly feel like Goliath must have felt the moment he realized he'd been beaten by David. I look behind me, and Kalinda is still standing in the yard. She nods her encouragement, so I turn back to the little girl.

"Do you know if she lives here?"

She nods. I'm about to ask her if she knows when my

mother will be back, but before I can, a man comes out of a hall and walks toward us so quickly that for a moment I'm sure he's one of the things that no one else can see. With him comes the scent of boiled plantain and lemongrass tea. I haven't eaten anything but Vienna sausages since yesterday, so the scents make me feel a little dizzy.

"Can I help you?" the man asks. He puts his hands on the girl's shoulders.

"Yes. I'm looking for Doreen Murphy."

He eyes me. "You're looking for Doreen Murphy," he repeats slowly.

I nod, and I expect for him to say where I can find her, but he keeps looking at me. "You're Doreen's daughter," he says.

I just stand there. I'm not sure what else to do or what to say. With the way he said my mom's name, and the way the little girl just keeps looking up at me with her big eyes, I'm not sure that there's anything to say. The man tells the girl to go set up the table, so she turns and runs, looking over her shoulder at me once before she disappears down the hall.

"Doreen wouldn't want you here," he says.

I feel my chest tighten. That's a cruel thing for him to say. "I just want to see her. I just want to talk to her."

"And say what?" he asks. He looks at me, and from the way he does, I think he might feel bad about his words. He isn't being mean or cruel on purpose—only truthful. I can hardly blame him for telling the truth. "She told me she doesn't want to meet with you if you ever end up coming here."

It's at that precise moment that a car comes up behind me and down the dirt path. The man clenches his jaw, but he doesn't try to make me or Kalinda leave. The car door opens and slams shut, and a woman comes, holding a bag of groceries. She doesn't notice me at first, but then she looks up and sees me and slows down.

Her face hasn't changed. I think her voice must be the same too.

Why you wanna fly, Blackbird?

My mother drops the groceries and puts a hand up to her mouth, and her hair is exactly the way I remember it—soft and curly and shining brown in the sunlight—and I don't know what to say or do. She walks toward me and puts her arms around me and holds me tightly, and that's when I start to cry. I clench the back of her shirt and feel my chest shake and wish I could stop, because I would like to have shown her how much of a mature young lady I've grown into, but she's crying too and smoothing down my hair.

She pulls away, wiping her eyes, and asks me to come inside. Kalinda stays standing there. She looks at me, and I know she doesn't want to follow me—she would rather wait out here. My mother picks up the bag of groceries, and the man opens the screen and stands to the side. She tells me his name is Richard. The little girl is back by the door, staring at us, wondering why we were crying. My mother picks her up and kisses her cheek. I envy this little girl more than I would have thought possible.

My mother leads me into the kitchen with the plantain and asks me if I'm hungry. Richard makes me a plate of plantain and oatmeal, since the salt fish is still stewing. I eat quietly, staring at her nose, her cheeks, her smile. I hadn't seen it before, when Kalinda told me that I resemble my mother, but I see it now. I see her in the same way I've seen my own reflection and stared at myself and barely recognized my own face—as if my bones had transformed overnight. She sits and sips tea and waits until Richard takes the little girl to the living room to watch cartoons. She smiles at me, and suddenly I can't look at her anymore.

"You're so beautiful," she says. "You look exactly like my cousin Idris when she was your age." She sips more tea.

"I always thought I looked more like my dad." I still can't look at her.

"You look like him too," she says. "You have his long arms and legs. But those eyes—those eyes definitely belong to my side of the family." She puts down her cup of tea. "I prayed for you. I prayed so hard for you, that you would be happy and be safe. I told Richard—I told him that I don't think I would ever forgive myself if anything had happened to you. I know that if I hadn't left, I would've made sure you stayed safe."

"My dad makes sure I'm safe."

She looks a little surprised that I'm defending my dad. "You're right. He does. He loves you very much."

I keep eating. I'm not so sure there's anything else I'm able to do.

She smiles a little and looks down at her tea. "I know that I've hurt you."

I don't say anything to this.

"I never wanted to hurt you. That was never my intention, Caroline."

I can't stop the questions that come from my mouth—the questions that I've been wanting to ask for so long, questions that might as well have existed since the beginning of time. "Then why did you leave?" And "Did you stop loving me?"

She's quiet for a long time now, and she takes a deep breath, and she isn't smiling anymore. "I'm going to tell you, because I think you're old enough to understand. I know you'll understand that I love you, no matter what. I look at you and think you remind me of when I was young. I think we might be similar. I liked to be alone a lot when I was younger, and I think you might be like that. Katie's more like her dad—she's shy when she just meets someone, but get her talking, and she'll never stop. But I think you're a lot like me, so I think you'll understand." She's quiet, because I can tell she doesn't really want to tell me, and her eyes are still wet.

"It's difficult to be the person I am in this world. I had a difficult time, living with who I was before."

I'm not sure what this means. "Who were you before?"

"I was a woman who was sure I didn't have a right to exist in this world," she says. "But now I know that I do. Just the same as anyone else. I have a right to exist and live and love and be loved."

She takes a breath. "And so do you, Caroline. I want you to know that more than anything else."

Hearing these words is like hearing permission to exist. I hadn't realized how badly I needed to hear this, and how important it would be to hear this from my mother. I can't help but smile, hearing her say this.

But it's not lost on me that she hasn't answered my questions—why she left, if she's stopped loving me— and these are the only things I care to hear about in the moment, the only things I can listen to her talk about right now. "If you wanted me to know this, then why didn't you stay to tell me for all the time you've been away?"

"Because I couldn't stay in that house anymore. Being in that house—it wasn't because of you. Understand that it had nothing to do with you. It didn't even have very much to do with your father. I was sad, Caroline. I was ill—sick, driving myself insane with loneliness."

I was always with her. I tell her this.

"I know," she says, "but it was a different kind of loneliness. A sort of loneliness I hope you never have to understand. I didn't leave you and your father," she tells me. "I'd tried to take my own life."

I can't understand these words, because I can't understand why she would ever want to hurt me in the worst way I could ever imagine. I'm angry at her. She's left me once before, but this—there would be no hope of her coming back to me, no chance that she would ever love me again. I'm furious at her for thinking of leaving me in that way. I'm angry at her for bringing me into this world, and then trying to leave me here alone.

"I'm sorry," she says, and I don't know if these are the last words she ever plans on speaking to me, but now I don't think I would mind if they are.

"I was taken to the hospital for treatment for some time, and when I was released, I decided not to go back to the house with you and your father. I knew then that this wasn't the life meant for me. I still know it now. Your father had Bernadette with another woman he loved, and I felt trapped. I couldn't breathe. I left—traveled the world and saw such amazing things. Things I want you to see for yourself someday too, Caroline. And when I came back, I met Richard, and I hadn't planned it at all, but I fell in love, and we got married. Katie is Richard's daughter, so she's my daughter now too. Katie is your stepsister."

She watches me for a moment, her mouth opening and closing, like she isn't sure if she should continue speaking or if she should wait for me to say something now.

"Do you love Katie more than you love me?"

"Love can't be measured."

"It can be when I'm your daughter."

"I love you very much, Caroline."

"Then why aren't you living with me? Why aren't you with my dad? Why are you with a new family?"

"I just wasn't happy. I didn't love your father, and he fell in love with another woman. I just wasn't happy."

I haven't finished eating yet, and my mother once taught me it was wrong to waste good food on the plate, but I ignore that now and stand up from the table so fast that the chair almost falls to the ground. My mom takes my hand before I can run.

"I've thought of coming to see you countless times," she says, "but I worried for myself—for my own health, worried that coming back would trigger something—and I worried about you too. I didn't want to hurt you." I yank my hand away from hers, and she lets go, but I stay standing at the table. "I've seen you," she says. "I've seen you on Main Street and crossing the street to the church to go to school and whenever you're walking past Frenchtown to get to waterfront."

We're quiet for a long while, and I hear rain lashing against the window, and my mother's new husband has turned on a radio. I can hear it faintly in the background. It says that the tropical storm is moving faster than anyone has really expected, and that it's quickly escalating. My mother tells me that she loves me, that she never stopped loving me.

Her new husband comes into the kitchen and invites me to stay a little longer, just to get to know everyone a little more—Katie wants to play board games with me, he says, but she's too shy to ask—but I can't imagine anything more painful than sitting here and pretending that my mother still loves me, that I'm a part of her new family, when in fact I'm only here because she and her new husband pity me. I tell them I have to go. Richard tells me he'll drive me home, but I tell them no, and I run out before anyone can say anything else.

If you'd only understand, dear.

When I race out onto the porch, screen door slapping shut behind me, I see that Kalinda is no longer standing where I'd left her, and something about this is not so surprising, because part of me wonders if she'd ever really been there at all.

Nobody wants you anywhere.

I run down the dirt path and back into the street, paved ground so hard it sends shock waves up my legs and into my knees, and I hear someone calling my name, and far down the road I see a woman dressed in all black, but I don't stop running, even then.

CHAPTER 11

The streets are near empty. Men playing their dominoes are gone, and someone's come and untied that dog from its chain. It's started to rain harder, the kind of lashing rain that stings when it hits your skin. Rain soaks me through even more than when I was in the ocean. And it's hot too—the unbearable kind of hot that makes it hard to breathe, and the wind blows into my face so hard I have to close my eyes, then it dies down, then it starts blowing again, like the island is breathing. One car comes by, slows down, and the man in the driving seat sticks his head out and yells at me to get home, I shouldn't be out in the street like this when the storm is coming. He drives on. Another car passes and stops, and a woman asks me if I need a ride, and when I lie and say my house is on the corner, she nods and keeps going.

I jump into a taxi that only has one other passenger, and when I jump off and don't pay, the driver doesn't cuss me. Mister Lochana isn't waiting for me on waterfront with his speedboat, so I get on the ferry to Water Island, which the ferry workers are saying will be the last ride for the day, since they'll need to anchor their boat at the dock and hope the boat doesn't end up in the middle of the road. Those workers don't cuss me when I don't pay, either; I guess because there's a storm coming and no one wants to cuss out a child right before a storm, else spirits will come and get them good.

I don't go home. I go walking down the road, streams of water running down like rivers, and keep walking through the mangroves, rain pelting against the tops of the trees, brown water swirling around my legs and water sloshing to my knees. My boat is right where I left it, floating upright and waiting for me, ready for the journey.

You ain't got no one to hold you.

Don't know where I'll be going now, but I'm going to let the water take me there.

You ain't got no one to care.

I lie down in my father's boat and rest my hands

over my chest like so, and close my eyes, to listen to the water and the wind, and I think maybe this is really where I belong after all. Nowhere else wants little Caroline Murphy.

Boat starts swaying and rocking to and fro, and the rain hits me hard and cold, so much so the water runs up my nose and stings my eyes and I can't breathe, so I get scared I might die, and just as I'm gasping and sitting up, I see the boat has been drawn out to the ocean, farther than I even really wanted it to. The waves are swelling with every second, and the black clouds in the sky fall down all around me. I can't see the lights of the island anymore. My heart is beating fast. I try sticking my arm into the water to paddle back, but I don't even know which direction to try and go in. I lean over too far and one wave comes and sucks me into the sea.

It's dark and quiet. Can only hear a beating in my heart. Spots of light shine through the gray water, specks swirling all around me. I can't see anything. I can't see the bottom. I try swimming for the top again, but another wave crashes down on me. I try reaching for the boat, but it's gone in a split second, gone so fast it might as well not even exist at all. My lungs are burning, and if I could cry I would, because my legs and arms are tired from all the kicking. Now I'm going to die. I'm going to die, and I'm going to leave my father behind. He won't have anyone anymore. Maybe that's what makes me the saddest of all.

Even light stops shining through, and everything's so dark that I almost don't see her. And there's my woman in black. Waiting for me like she's been waiting my whole life. Come like she's ready to take me away now. Nothing I can do about that. I just close my eyes.

*

I can breathe. My throat feels raw whenever I do, but I still take in one long breath and let it out slowly, savoring the feeling of air in my lungs. There's yellow light pressing against my eyelids. I open them, and I see I'm in a bed that's not my own, in a room of white walls and one single window with open curtains and a closed door.

My father is there, but he isn't looking at me. He's sitting in a chair with his head resting in his hands, bent over like he's been that way since the day I left. Maybe I let out air a little differently than before, because something catches his attention. He looks up and stands up, and for a second it looks like he isn't sure if he wants to cry or hug me or slap me, and maybe it's possible for him to do all at once, but he doesn't do any of them, so I tell him that I'm sorry. He nods and pats my hand uncertainly, like he still doesn't know if he wants to hit me, but then he finally wraps his arms around me and holds me tightly and shakes as he cries like a little boy might cry in his own mother's arms. His voice rumbles low, like he hasn't spoken in years, and he tells me never to do that to him again, before asking me if I'm feeling all right, if I need anything at all, and saying that I should never do anything like that ever again.

I tell him I'm fine about a dozen times before he believes me, even though I don't know if I believe myself. I'm too afraid to ask my father what I think might be the truth. That I might have actually died, and that he's a figment of my imagination in a personalized heaven. Though maybe it's a little much to think I'd actually be in heaven.

I decide to tell him the truth. "I went to see my mother."

"I know," he says. "I got a phone call from her. She said that you'd found her."

"You knew she was here."

He doesn't answer me. I wish I could be angry at him, the way I know I should feel, but I think I'm just too tired to feel much of anything. My lungs are still burning, my throat raw, and my legs and arms are the sorest they've ever been.

"Why didn't you tell me?"

He swallows hard. "I didn't think you'd understand— didn't want to scare you. She mentioned she told you the truth," he says. "She tried to hurt herself, and she needed the space, but I . . . I thought it might be easier to say she'd just left us than to explain everything. I'm sorry. I should've told you the truth."

We sit in quiet for another long while, partly because I have too many thoughts swirling through my head to grasp one and put a voice to it, and partly because my throat still hurts too much anyway.

"How was she?" he asks me.

What sort of question is that? How in the world could I ever answer something like that? "I don't know," I tell him. "She seemed happy."

He sighs. "It doesn't mean she doesn't love us, Caroline."

"No. It means she doesn't love you."

"Now, you don't mean that."

No, I didn't mean it, but I'm more angry than tired now, and I don't feel like telling him the truth anymore.

"You scared the hell out of me," he says. "You know that?"

I decide to grace him with a glance. He takes my hand and doesn't let go even when I've looked away again. "What happened?" I ask. The curiosity is too much not to ask.

"Mister Lochana found you washed up on shore," he says. "He thought you had—well..." he says, looking away. "He got me and we brought you to the hospital."

"Then that's the second time Mister Lochana has rescued me," I say—but I think of the woman in black, waiting for me beneath the waves.

My father doesn't say anything for some time. He only sits and holds my hand. "Your mom and I both love you very much. We made mistakes—but we tried to do the best we could."

"I know." And I do know. I know he tried, and he's still trying, and he'll still make mistakes sometimes, because he's a human being, and I've learned now that this is what human beings are always destined to do. Including me. I tell him that I love him, and he smiles like that's the best news he's heard all day and puts an arm around me and kisses the side of my head. He tells me that my mother has come to visit a few times. He asks me if it'd be all right, if she came in to see me. I tell him absolutely not—it would never be all right. He just kisses the side of my head again.

*

I stay in the hospital for an entire two days before they allow me to leave once again. The island of Saint Thomas has been battered. The ten-dollar ferry is in the middle of the road, and palm trees have fallen to the side.

People walk in the street, cleaning up clutter. My father has tied his blue boat to waterfront. He hasn't touched that boat in over one year and six months now. It bobs up and down with every passing wave. We step onto it, and he rows me across the clear blue water, the way he used to when I was a child. I think I might still be a child now, after all.

Our house is still standing, the same way it always has been. Maybe the storm couldn't see us here on Water Island either. We go inside, and absolutely nothing has changed, which is disappointing and thrilling all at the same time. My father tells me that my mother has called again. That she wants to reconnect with me—be a part of my life.

"Well, she shouldn't have left my life at all." That's what I say to that.

My father only nods like he agrees.

*

I'm eating breakfast at the table when my father sits down beside me with the mail. He opens each letter individually, and my heart begins to beat faster despite itself, even though I already know there won't be any postcards in the pile. My father picks up one letter, then pauses—and stretches out his hand to me.

"It's for you."

I look from the letter to him, then reach out to take it carefully. This is the first mail I've ever received. I think it must be a practical joke. But then I read the corner address, and see that the letter was sent from Kalinda Francis from a town in Barbados.

I hold the letter with shaking hands.

"Aren't you going to open it?" he asks.

I almost shake my head and hand the letter back to him. How easy that would've been, to not have to read a single word sent by Kalinda Francis. But instead, I nod and scrape my chair back and excuse myself from the table, walking to my room and closing the door. I open Kalinda's letter and read it quickly first, eyes flashing over her jumble of words, before going back to the beginning once again. The letter says:

My dearest Caroline, I've agonized over the way I left you, but I couldn't bear the thought of saying good-bye. I was too afraid. Will you ever forgive me? I'm back home with my mother and my seven siblings. my father has continued his carpentry. my mother claims that she will never let me leave her sight again. This makes me happy, and it also makes me so happy that you've been able to meet your mother again. This was at least a happy ending, wasn't it? I so wish that ours could've been a happy ending as well. But maybe it still can be, one day. I love you, and I will continue to love you forever, and even if we never see each other again and when we're fully grown adults and I have married someone else, I'll think back to the time I spent on Saint Thomas and fell in love with Caroline murphy. I hope you can think of me in the same way, and when you remember me, you only think about how you'd fallen in love with kalinda

Francis. But even as I write now, I can't help but think that it would be an atrocity to let our ending come like this. I'm on Barbados, and you're on Water Island, but we're both still alive. Think about how amazing that is, Caroline. An infinite number of universes and an infinite amount of time, and we were able to meet each other. We could have been born millions of years apart, but we were able to meet each other and fall in love. That's a true miracle, isn't it? Maybe it doesn't have to end this way.

I'm not surprised by any of these words. I expected her to tell me that she loves me, and that she misses me, and that she wishes she were still on Saint Thomas, and that she was sorry. She couldn't bear the thought of saying good-bye. She was too afraid. But she hopes she will one day see me again.

Will you write to me, Caroline?

I nod, and fold the letter neatly, and put it on my dressing table. I'll have to find a lot of paper and many pens.

*

My father tells me at dinner that my mother has called for me again.

"Can't she realize I don't want to speak to her?"

"But she wants to speak to you."

"I don't care."

"She loves you very much, Caroline. She made a mistake. She wants you back in her life."

"It's too late for that now, right?"

My father doesn't answer. He can't look at me.

"Isn't it too late?"

"I told her to come over," he says.

I get up from my chair and walk to my room and slam the door shut and lock it. My father doesn't even try to ask me to come back outside. I hear voices, and I hear my mother, but I stay right where I am.

CHAPTER
12

I return to school, and nothing has changed there either, except the fact that Kalinda is gone, and I am now alone once more. Anise takes particular pleasure in this. I'd made the mistake of thinking that perhaps we'd grown closer, and were no longer enemies, since she was not torturing me for the past week—but perhaps she had only stopped because of Kalinda. Now that Kalinda is no longer here, everything goes back to the way it was. Anise begins talking loudly about me, the smelly sinner, and in class often asks Missus Wilhelmina if I should even be allowed to go to this school. Missus Wilhelmina always agrees that sinners should be expelled, but says it's out of her control, most unfortunately.

The group of hyenas laugh along with Anise, as always—but I can't help but notice that Marie Antoinette isn't laughing. Not one bit. She doesn't even break a smile. It comes to the point where, one day passing by her lunch table, I hear Anise ask, "What is wrong with you, Marie Antoinette?"

And she doesn't answer, of course, because that's another thing that hasn't changed—Marie Antoinette still won't say a single word—but sometimes, when I catch her staring at me, I think she has much more to say than anyone else around.

*

After Kalinda, I find it difficult to come back to sitting in complete silence. My loneliness will sooner kill me than the ocean will. So finally, I must give in. I accept Miss Joe's invitation to eat lunch in her office.

She has cleared some piles of papers and books from her desk, though the photos in their frames are still in their line. "It was getting a bit too messy in here, wouldn't you agree?"

I decide it's more polite not to say anything at all. I eat my food quietly, still angry at the woman sitting across from me, but happy that at least I'm not sitting alone.

"I heard from Doreen that you visited her," she says.

I look at her. "You still speak to her?"

"Oh, yes," she says. "Remember? We speak on birthdays and every Christmas. It was my birthday last weekend, you know."

I don't even want to wish her a happy birthday. She smiles at me, waiting. I cut my eye and sigh. "Happy belated birthday."

"Why, thank you, Miss Murphy," she says. She dips her spoon into a container of chicken dumpling soup, swimming in grease. She slurps. "She told me it was a difficult time. For both of you."

"A difficult time, for her? She isn't the one that got abandoned."

"It's so easy to be self-involved when you're young." She laughs. "Don't look at me like you want to kill me, now. I can't help the truth. You don't know anything about your mother's hardships. She made many mistakes, yes—there's no question in that. I'm not defending her choices. But I can understand them." She turns her head to the side, and I feel like I'm in a classroom. "Can you?"

She leaves me with that question for the day, and I roll it around in my mind all night and well into the morning too. When I go to her office the next day for lunch, I expect her to ask it again, and I'm ready with my answer—prepared to say that I do understand, even though I don't agree with any of it, even though I'm still angry at my mother for everything. But Miss Joe doesn't even ask. She tells me to speak to her about my adventures leading up to finding my mother instead.

So I tell her everything. About looking for evidence, and even about sneaking into this very office, because something tells me she already knows about her missing photograph anyway. I tell her about Kalinda, and the journal that Anise found—about us running away and the condo. I tell her about the woman in black.

"The woman in black?" she says.

"Yes. That's what I call her."

"Describe her to me."

That's what I do. "She's been around since I was a young child."

She nearly laughs. "You're still a child, Miss Murphy." Her smile fades. "And you believe in spirits, do you?"

I almost tell her Kalinda's warning—that the spirits will hear her calling their name—but I stop myself. There's much more in this life to fear than just spirits, and if I let fear rule my every move, I will become nothing more than a little ghost child myself. I want to be brave. I want to live the life I was given. So what if the spirits hear us call their names? Let them hear it.

"Yes. I do believe in spirits."

Miss Joe is thinking hard about something. "What do you think of the woman in black?"

"I don't know," I admit. "I thought for a long time she was a demon. I thought she'd stolen my mother at first. She scared me. I thought she wanted me dead."

"And now?"

I think of the ocean, the darkness—feeling her there with me. The bubbles as large as my mom's head, the coral scratching my knees. The shadows of my bedroom when I've told myself I don't matter enough to be in this world. Rocks digging through my shoes as I run through wind and rain, black chasing me through the storm. Sitting patiently on my father's boat, moon eyes gazing at me, like she's always been there, and always will be. A memory I did not know I had comes to me. Beneath the waves, sucked beneath, the feel of her warm grasp. She pulled me from the sea. She's always been with me. She's always protected me.

"You believe in spirits," Miss Joe says, "but do you believe in guardian angels?" She smiles at the look on my face. "I think there's always something out there watching over us—making sure we're safe and loved. You're very lucky, Caroline."

This is the first time Miss Joe has ever said my given name, and that makes me nice and surprised—but even after the lunch bell rings, and well through class, and back on the speedboat with Mister Lochana, listening to him speak about the days when he was a little boy and working on his father's farm, I can't stop thinking about the woman in black. My own spirit, watching over me. I stare beneath the waves, half expecting to see her now, though I don't.

When I get home, my father is sitting on the sofa. He's been home much more since I almost drowned in his boat. He is holding a photo of Bernadette and a letter with large cursive handwriting from the little girl.

My father says that when she came here to meet him, he was too afraid to introduce us but that Bernadette will now come to Water Island every summer so I can get to know my half sister even more. I'm surprised, because I realize that I would like this very much, and I realize that I would like something else very much too.

"Daddy," I say, and when I say this word, it really is with love this time.

"Yes, Caroline?"

"I'm ready to see my mother again."

He doesn't hesitate to pick up the phone.

*

The door opens, and there she is. My mother walks into the house that had once been her home, wearing a blue dress, with her hair brown and curled. She looks like she might as well have never left.

The first time I saw her, I didn't want to look at her, but I do now. She looks even older than I remember her, and that makes me sad, and she has laugh lines and wrinkles around her eyes, which makes me happy too.

She smiles at my dad and asks him how he is, and

they have a boring conversation about work and the weather, in the way that adults feel like they always must, and then my dad looks at me to make sure I'm all right before he decides to leave us alone. He walks outside to stand in the road. I sit on the chair opposite my mother, who sits on the sofa. I feel like I'm the parent, about to reprimand her. She sits with her hands pressed together.

She tells me that she works in the post office, and that her mother, my grandmother, passed away of breast cancer seven months before, and that Katie won't stop asking about me, keeps on asking to see me. "She's really a sweet girl."

I clench my hands together. "I'm not sweet at all."

"No," she says. "You're not. But that's what I love about you. I'm not sweet either. I think you got that from me."

"I'm not like you. I would never leave my own daughter."

"That's the problem with growing up, Caroline. You're not sure what you will and won't do anymore."

I'm so angry I could cry. I am crying a little, but it's embarrassing to cry in front of her, and it makes me even angrier, because she's the reason I'm crying in the first place, and I don't want her to know how much she's hurt me—that she's cut right into me, and that even after this past year, even when she's gone on to love a new daughter and have another family, I've just been cut and bleeding and trying not to cry.

"I love you. You have to know that."

And what frustrates me most is that I do know that.

She gets a little quiet, then says, "I spoke to Richard, and we—Caroline, we'd love it if we could be in your life. I know that isn't fair to ask, since we decided we wouldn't be, but if you can forgive us—that's more than I deserve, but I hope you can forgive us. Katie would love it too. I know this isn't the family most people have, but we love you, and I love you so much, and that's all that a family needs, really. I'd love to be in your life, if you'll let me."

She's watching me, and I'm sure her heart has stopped dead in her chest. She waits for me to speak.

"Why do you love the song 'Blackbird'?" I ask.

She watches me. "What?"

"The song. 'Blackbird,' by Nina Simone. Why do

you love it so much? When you were home, you would sing it all the time. You never stopped singing it."

She wipes her cheeks. "Oh, I—I don't know." She pauses to think. "It captured how I felt at one time in my life, perfectly. It was the song for one era of my life. But that era has passed now. I can look at that time and listen to that song and appreciate that this is what I've come from—but I can also recognize how I've changed. Does that make any sense?"

It's scary, because it makes more sense than I ever thought it would. I nod. "Yes."

She doesn't understand at first, so I say, "Yes, I'd like you back in my life again."

CHAPTER
13

I haven't seen the woman in black in a long while. Not in a few months, in fact. It used to scare me, even thinking about the chance of seeing her—but now when I think about her, I can't help but feel a peace surging beneath my skin. I still don't really know who the woman in black is—if she's my guardian angel, if she's an ancestor from my past or my future—but I know that she'll always be with me. That's the most important part of all.

Days and weeks and months pass, and I'm now in a new era of my life. Nothing about it is perfect, but things have changed so much, and suddenly I'm thirteen years old and I'm in my last year of school in the church with Missus Wilhelmina and Jesus hanging on his cross, before I have to start high school in the countryside.

Anise Fowler moves to a different island, and the

pack of hyenas slowly separates, and suddenly I find that I'm sitting at lunch tables where there are other people. I'm not sitting with them, but I'm sitting near them, and that's different too.

One day I walk into the cafeteria and see Marie Antoinette sitting alone. She's sat alone the last few times I've seen her. I can't help but wonder why. I walk across the cafeteria, loafers sticking to the yellow tile, until I'm right in front of Marie Antoinette. She looks up at me and stares.

"Can I sit here?" I ask.

She nods.

I sit down, my tray clattering. I don't eat. I just sit and watch while she sits and watches me. "Why don't you ever have anything to say?" I ask.

She gives me a confused look.

"You never speak," I say. "It's like you're mute. You refuse to say a single word."

"That's because no one's ever listening," she says. It's the first time I'm hearing her voice, and it comes out loud and strong and powerful, like she's a second away from beginning to yell. I almost fall off my seat in surprise. But she only smiles. "You don't talk very much at all either, you know."

This is surprising. "I talk all the time."

"No, you don't," she says after a second of looking me up and down. "But maybe you think that you do. I think that's interesting."

"You didn't seem to think it was so interesting when you and your friends treated me the way you did."

"Anise Fowler wasn't my friend," she says. "She hated me the most of all. She'd sit with me just so she could torture me. I let it happen for a long time. But then I changed. I had a pretty eventful year, you know."

I have to smile. "I can't wait to hear all about it, then."

Acknowledgments

It takes a village to create a book, and I'm lucky enough to have had the support of many:

Beth Phelan, rock star agent, who championed and helped shape the seed of *Hurricane Child*.

Legendary editor Andrea Pinkney, whose vision helped make *Hurricane Child* what it is today, along with the rest of the amazing Scholastic crew: David Levithan, Kait Feldmann, Natalia Remis, Deimosa Webber-Bay, Lizette Serrano, Lauren Donovan, Michelle Campbell, Emily Heddleson, Baily Crawford, Melissa Schirmer, Rachel Gluckstern, and Angelique Browne, along with artist Tonya Engel, who made the book come to life with a beautiful cover.

My friends, who gave invaluable feedback and support: Nikki Garcia, Hayley Chewins, Shannon Rogers, Jennifer Poe, and Katherine Webber.

And above all else, my family: especially my dad, Caswil Callender, and Auntie Jacqui, who have always believed in me, and who I think of when I'm not so sure of myself. And my mom, Barbara Callwood, who has read every piece of writing and heard every tearful monologue about my fears and uncertainties on whether I'll ever see one of my books published, and has forever remained unflinching in her belief that I one day would.

AFTER WORDS™

KACEN CALLENDER'S

Hurricane Child

CONTENTS

About the Author

Born and raised on St. Thomas of the US Virgin Islands, Kacen Callender holds a BA from Sarah Lawrence College, where they studied fine arts, Japanese, and creative writing, as well as an MFA from The New School's Writing for Children program. Their debut novel, *Hurricane Child*, was the winner of the 2019 Stonewall Book Award and the 2019 Lambda Literary Award for LGBTQ Children's/Young Adult, as well as a Kirkus Best Book of 2018. Their forthcoming novel, *King and the Dragonflies*, is a dreamy and emotional story of a boy living near the bayous of Louisiana that reminds us love will help us weather any storm. Kacen spends their free time playing video games and watching anime and reality TV shows. They currently live and write in Philadelphia.

Q&A with Kacen Callender

Q: *How did the idea for this book come about? Was any of it drawn from your own life?*

A: Yes, *Hurricane Child* was strongly based on my own life! Like Caroline, I'm a hurricane child: someone who is born during or within a few days of a hurricane. I was born two days after Hurricane Hugo, which had been previously the most destructive hurricane to hit the US Virgin Islands, before Hurricanes Irma and Maria in 2017. Being a hurricane child, I was told growing up that I bring bad luck, which was easy to believe, since my birthdays are usually around the time of hurricanes—but like Caroline, I also struggled a lot with identity, bullying, and feeling isolated. I wanted to write a novel for young readers who might be struggling with the same things I did.

Q: *What was your favorite part of St. Thomas that you got to include in* Hurricane Child? *What made you want to write a story based there?*

A: My favorite part that I included of St. Thomas, and all of the US Virgin Islands, really, is the beauty: the blue of the sky and sea, the cool trade wind breeze, the green hills and white sand, the houses of all colors, and the people. I don't get to go back home often, so imagining the beauty of the islands always helps me feel just a little less homesick. I wanted to write a story set in the US Virgin Islands because I've never seen a novel for young readers set there before. I wanted to write for young readers in the US Virgin Islands and the

Caribbean, but I also wanted to tell a story to show a world to young readers who've never seen a world like mine.

Q: *Does Water Island exist?*
A: It does! Water Island became the fourth official main island of the US Virgin Islands in 1996, and had even originally been a part of St. Thomas, before a strip of land connecting the two islands was destroyed to create a better water flow for St. Thomas's waterfront and docks.

Q: *One of the most interesting elements of the story is the woman in black, a spirit who appears to Caroline. What made you want to bring the supernatural into the story?*
A: Thank you! Yes, it was important for me to include the supernatural as an element of magical realism. The US Virgin Islands, and the Caribbean itself, feels like the genre of magical realism, where racism and oppression mix with the spirits that fill the islands and the sea. If you couldn't tell, I believe that ghosts are real, and absolutely believe that the Caribbean is incredibly haunted! The story wouldn't have felt true without a mention of the spirits.

Q: *What was it like writing for a community that is not often written about, especially by someone who has firsthand experience in it?*
A: There was some pressure, especially knowing that this was the only middle grade book set in the US Virgin Islands. I wanted people from the US Virgin Islands to read it and feel proud, and feel that the story was relatable and realistic to their experiences as well. I was also nervous because the

character, like me, is queer, and the islands haven't always been as accepting of LGBTQIA+ people. But the response overall has been positive!

Q: Hurricane Child *is your debut novel, and recently added the 2019 Stonewall Book Award to a growing list of accolades and honors. How does it feel to have such positive reception for this book?*

A: It's been uplifting and inspiring, and above all else, extremely validating—not only to myself as a writer, but to my identity as a queer black person from the Caribbean. I haven't often felt accepted by many communities, so to write about my experiences and my identities, and to win an award for doing so, felt like a metaphor of acceptance. I hope that these awards can mean we'll be able to see more books like *Hurricane Child,* featuring more queer people of color, by more queer authors of color. I'm excited to see what the future will bring!

Turn the page for a sneak peek at
Stonewall Book Award–winning author
Kacen Callender's latest book!

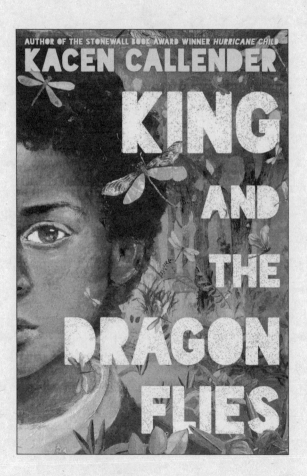

CHAPTER
1

The dragonflies live down by the bayou, but there's no way to know which one's my brother. There are hundreds, maybe even thousands, just sitting on tree branches and rocks, baking in the sun, flitting over the brown water that seeps up from the dirt, zipping across the sky, showing off their ghostlike wings. Happy in their own dragonfly paradise.

I want to ask Khalid—I want to ask him, "Why did you choose a dragonfly? Why not something cooler, like a lion or a panther or a wolf?" And if he were still in the body that's now buried in the ground over in the Richardson cemetery, he might hit me upside the head with his crooked grin and say, "Let me alone. I can choose to be whatever I want." And I wouldn't be able to argue, because I know he'd be exactly right about that.

*

I like to look for my brother in the afternoon by the bayou, on the long and hot and sweaty walk back from school, down the hard dirt road that weaves between the thorny bushes with their big fluffy leaves, and through the trees with their moss and vines, cicadas making their noise and birds whistling their tunes. Those trees always seem to be watching. Like they've got a secret to tell me, if only I'd stop for a second and wait and listen. Or it could be the ghosts. Just as my mom says: "Plenty of ghosts here in Louisiana watching your every move, so you best mind yourself."

I'm doing exactly that—just minding myself, kicking away some stones whenever they're in my path, thinking on my brother and dragonflies and the world and the universe, because it can be funny sometimes, thinking about how small we are no matter what body we're in—when there's a crunching behind me. I turn and look to see a rusting white pickup coming, kicking up dust behind it, so I step to the side of the road and onto the browning grass, expecting it to zoom by, but the pickup slows down until it stops right beside me. There're a few white boys inside, but my heart drops into my stomach when I see the driver. Mikey Sanders.

He was in my brother's class. He hated my brother. My brother hated him. But most people do, on account of the fact that Mikey Sanders helped kill a man. No one says it because of who his father is—no one will admit in the courtroom that the older Sanders boy helped three other murderers beat a black man to death and then drag him all around the bayou. But everyone knows it was Mikey Sanders's white pickup truck that did the dragging. Same truck he's driving now, right here in front of me.

He's got a sunburn across his face and tiny blue eyes and pale hair, so pale it might as well be white, too. He's smoking a cigarette even though I know he isn't yet eighteen, and he wears a collared shirt like he's just come back from church.

My brother and Mikey got into fights—and I mean real throw-'em-down fistfights. My brother said Mikey's a racist, that Mikey called him the N-word and made monkey noises and would leave bananas on his desk.

Even tied up a T-shirt like a noose and put it in my brother's gym locker. It's not surprising, I guess, given Mikey Sanders is the grandson of Gareth Sanders, who was a member of the white sheet–wearing KKK. And now Mikey Sanders is here, looking at me like he's thinking of dragging me from the back of his pickup truck, too.

He doesn't say anything for a long moment. Just looks me up and down, his truck's engine still rumbling and shaking, almost as much as I'm trembling on my feet. His friends in the passenger seat and the back seat are as silent as stones.

Mikey flicks his cigarette to the ground and sucks on his teeth. I flinch, and I know how I must look to him. I look scared—like I'm about to wet my pants. I don't care, because that's exactly what I am: as scared as the day I was born and pushed out wailing into this world. I was scared to be alive then, and I'm scared I'm going to die now.

Mikey finally speaks. "Sorry about your brother," he says.

I don't answer him. I don't know if he's serious, if he's joking, or if he's just being plain mean.

He shrugs, like he can hear all my questions and he doesn't know any of the answers himself. "What're you doing out here?" he says, eyes scanning the trees all around me.

I still don't say a single word. Is he trying to figure out if I'm on this road by myself? Trying to see if he can get away with killing me, too?

He looks my way again, still sucking his teeth. Must be a piece of food stuck way in there. "We're headed into town." He rubs his nose. "Want to hop in the back?"

Something possesses me and I'm able to move. I shake my head once, hard and fast.

Mikey shifts in his seat. "You know, your brother—" I'm not sure what he's going to say, and maybe he isn't so sure either, because he stops himself right there. "See you around."

And he peels off, turning back onto the road and racing out of sight, leaving a cloud of dust behind him. I stand right where I am, taking one long shaky breath, and wait until my heart slows down. What would my dad say if he saw me as scared as this? What would my brother say?

I know what my brother would say. "No way you can live your life as a coward. If you're always too busy hiding, then you're not really living, are you?"

I take in another long breath and keep on walking.

*

The dirt road becomes rocky with gravel and then becomes paved, and I'm right where I'm supposed to be, walking by my neighborhood's collection of silver trailers and one-story paneled houses and windows with the blinds and curtains closed, rusting cars and trucks shimmering under the sun and collecting all the light in the world and bouncing it right into my eyes. It's hot. It's always hot in Louisiana, but today it feels like the devil came up out of his grave. I'm sweating from every pore as I walk, my socks squishy and my shirt sticking to my back. My bag is empty, but it feels like a ton of stones weighing down my shoulders.

My mom and dad's house is at the end of a long road, farther away from everyone else, with walls of chipping white paint and a front yard of dead yellow grass. I stomp up the steps and grab my key from my backpack. It used to be Khalid's key. It's copper, like a faded penny. Khalid's hands were bigger than mine as they reached into his bag and pulled out the key after our walk home from school under the same sky, same heat, same everything as before, except for the fact that Khalid is now gone. He'd unlock the door, and the two of us would fall into the shade, scrambling over each other to get to the TV remote first. Khalid almost always won our race just to show he could, but then most times he'd let me watch whatever I wanted to anyway.

Dim light swirls in through the windows and the gauzy curtains. The living room is all wood—wood-paneled walls, wood-paneled floors—and furniture that's too big for the space, with plastic covering my dad's favorite sitting chair. My mom's been saying we need to redecorate for years, and I think she might've done it, too, but now these days she mostly sits and stares, hand on her chin—until she snaps out of it and looks up with this smile. My mom's smile drives me up the wall sometimes. I know it's fake. She knows it's fake. So why does she always pretend to smile?

My mom's still at work at the post office, and my dad's still at work at the construction site, so I'm alone now, trying not to remember the way Khalid would be stretched out on the couch, falling asleep with his phone in his hand. The TV is on to some afternoon rerun of an anime show, and I'm just sitting on the couch where Khalid used to sit, staring and blinking and thinking. What was Mikey Sanders going to say about my brother?

Does Mikey know my brother's a dragonfly?

It happened at the funeral. We were in the front row of the overheated church. Someone was crying behind me. Most were swatting their programs to push away the heat. My dad used to tell me all the time that boys don't cry, but sitting there that day, his face was wet, salted water dripping from his eyes, off his nose and chin, and he didn't bother wiping his face, didn't bother trying to hide it. I didn't even know so much water could be inside a person—like he was hiding an entire ocean beneath his skin.

My mom's hands were clenched, hard, around a crumpled-up piece of tissue in her lap, and she was staring without blinking, her eyes wide—staring right at where my brother's old body was lying in his casket. I know most folks like to say a dead person looks like they're sleeping, but I didn't think so. I know what my brother looked like when he was asleep. He was always dreaming. Always smirking, or frowning at something I couldn't see, outright laughing before he mumbled and turned over, some nights even speaking to me. We shared the same bed in our cramped little room, and sometimes I'd kick him just so that he'd shut up and let me sleep, too, but other times I'd sit and curl my knees to my chest and listen. He'd mostly say things that made no sense, or speak so low I couldn't hear what he was telling me—but sometimes he'd whisper secrets about the universe. It was almost like he was given a special ticket to see a magic world in his dreams, even if he couldn't remember anything when he woke up.

That boy lying there in that casket wasn't asleep. He wasn't even my brother. He was like a snake's second skin, shed off and forgotten and empty on the ground. I was mad that day. Why would we sit here crying over some forgotten skin? It's like mourning a moth's cocoon. If

Khalid had seen us there crying over that old body of his, what would he had done?

My brother could slip into a whole other universe in his sleep. *We're all made of light.*

That's all I could think about, when just as the choir began to sing, a dragonfly flew in through a window—and I know those wings must've been going a mile a minute, but it was like they slowed down somehow, those crystal patterns shimmering and shining. The dragonfly's green little body and big eyes floated right past me and landed on the edge of the casket.

I'd sat up in our bed all night sometimes, listening to my brother as he told me about the other worlds he could see.

There's a purple sky, King. There are mushrooms as tall as trees. I have dragonfly wings.

Discover SCHOLASTIC GOLD for exclusive bonus content!

SCHOLASTIC

scholastic.com/ScholasticGold